"You're wasted in the job!" Khalid drawled

And Lorna retorted, "I hope your next remark isn't going to be, 'What's a nice girl like you doing in a job like this?' "

"That's exactly what I was going to say!" Khalid continued, "To break the monotony, how about a trip to Paris or Rome for a few days?"

One look into his deep blue eyes was sufficient for Lorna to understand the full implication of his invitation. Khalid wanted her, but not in the way she had hoped.

"You disappoint me," she said, hiding her anger. "I expected a little more finesse than that. My answer is no!"

But her heart pounded. She mustn't let him know how deeply she was attracted to him. Khalid wanted a diversion—she wanted marriage or nothing!

WELCOME
TO THE WONDERFUL WORLD
OF *Harlequin Romances*

Interesting, informative and entertaining,
each Harlequin Romance portrays an appealing
and original love story. With a varied array
of settings, we may lure you on an African safari,
to a quaint Welsh village, or an exotic Riviera
location—anywhere and everywhere that adventurous
men and women fall in love.

As publishers of Harlequin Romances, we're
extremely proud of our books. Since 1949,
Harlequin Enterprises has built its publishing
reputation on the solid base of quality and
originality. Our stories are the most popular
paperback romances sold in North America; every
month, six new titles are released and sold at
nearly every book-selling store in Canada and the
United States.

A free catalogue listing all Harlequin Romances
can be yours by writing to the

HARLEQUIN READER SERVICE,
(In the U.S.) 1440 South Priest Drive, Tempe, AZ 85281
(In Canada) Stratford, Ontario, N5A 6W2

We sincerely hope you enjoy reading
this Harlequin Romance.

Yours truly,

THE PUBLISHERS
Harlequin Romances

No Time for Love

by

KAY CLIFFORD

Harlequin Books

TORONTO • LONDON • LOS ANGELES • AMSTERDAM
SYDNEY • HAMBURG • PARIS • STOCKHOLM • ATHENS • TOKYO

Original hardcover edition published in 1980
by Mills & Boon Limited

ISBN 0-373-02468-1

Harlequin edition published April 1982

CHAPTER ONE

RICHARD PALFREY seated himself behind his large, leather-topped desk and gave his patient a reassuring smile. Lorna Masters was a beautiful girl despite the fact that she was now reed-thin, and had dark circles beneath her widely-spaced violet eyes that no amount of make-up could hide. As he watched her, she tugged at a lock of corn-coloured hair and leaned forward in her seat, impatiently waiting for his diagnosis.

'Don't look so worried,' he said. 'There's nothing physically wrong with you. Just a bad case of overwork.'

'That's impossible.' The girl's voice was soft and gave no indication of her strong character. 'I've only been back at the hospital a month.'

'A month too soon. You shouldn't have gone back yet. You had a severe bout of pneumonia and I warned you this might happen if you did.'

'They were so short-staffed I couldn't stay away any longer.'

'Your first duty is to yourself.' The specialist frowned. 'You need a much easier job for the moment. Go into private nursing for a while. I can refer you to several of my patients who'd be delighted to have you.'

Lorna made a face. 'I don't fancy playing nursemaid to some rich hypochondriac.'

'It isn't only the poor who are ill,' he pointed out.

'I know. And I apologise for my answer. It was silly.'

He shrugged. 'I'll leave the type of job to you. But make sure it isn't as demanding as your present one. You know what overwork did to your father.' Dr Palfrey rubbed the side of his nose. 'How is he these days?'

'Not too bad—considering he's had two heart attacks. He still sees a few patients at home.'

'You never thought of following in his footsteps the way your brother did?'

'No. I always wanted to be a nurse like my mother.'

'Where is Allan now?' he asked.

'In the Middle East.' Lorna's eyes, fringed by long curling lashes, sparkled for the first time as she spoke of her brother's career. 'He's head of gynaecology at a large new hospital. Working out there he's been able to advance far more quickly than he would have done in England.'

'No doubt,' Dr Palfrey commented a trifle cynically. 'Let's hope he can obtain the same sort of position when he returns home.'

Driving back to the hospital in her second-hand Mini, Lorna knew she would have to take the specialist's advice. She should have convalesced for at least a month longer. But she loved her work too much to enjoy idleness and, after her recent promotion, had still been basking in the glory of being the youngest sister at St Matthew's. How irritated Matron would be when she asked for leave of absence to take an easier position!

But to her surprise, Matron took it well, only showing concern for her recovery.

'I'd rather lose you on a temporary basis than lose you completely—which is what will happen if you don't take a break. When do you want to leave?'

'Dr Palfrey thinks it should be at once.'

'Then do as he says.'

For the next week Lorna continued with her usual routine at the hospital, but in her free time she went for several interviews. There was no shortage of easy, well-paid jobs, but she did not find one she cared to accept, and it was Ann Henderson, her flatmate, who nursed at a private clinic in Harley Street, who finally found something which she thought would be suitable and telephoned her in great excitement at eight o'clock one evening to tell her about it.

'One of our nurses recently accepted a job as nanny with a fabulously rich Arab family who are living over here, but she's just being wheeled off for an emergency gall bladder op. and won't be able to take it. The pay's marvellous and there are masses of perks, so you'd better telephone straight away.'

'I don't fancy looking after a brood of children,' Lorna answered doubtfully. 'And why the rush? Tell me about it in the morning. I'm going out with David and we're already late.'

'There's no brood of children—only a baby—and if you don't call now, half the staff here will be after it when they find Maggie can't take it. For goodness' sake at least see them.'

Lorna wrote down the number she was to call, then looked apologetically at the red-haired man seated opposite her on the couch. He had followed the gist of the conversation and he pointed to the telephone.

'The quicker you make the call, the quicker we can go out to dinner.'

Lorna gave him a grateful smile. David Tindell was a pleasant young man with an easy charm and a slightly stiff personality that no amount of teasing could ease. Nearly six feet tall, with neat features and slate-grey eyes, he was attractive to most women, yet made it obvious that he had eyes only for Lorna. She had known him for several years, for he had trained at the same hospital as her brother, though it was not until Allan had accepted a job in Kuwait that they had started dating.

'Phone them,' he repeated. 'If it's as good a job as Ann says, you won't want to miss it.'

A few moments later the call was completed. Lorna had been unable to speak to Madam Rashid who was in bed and had left orders not to be disturbed, but her husband had arranged for her to come for an interview the following afternoon.

'Now you'll be able to concentrate on *me* for the evening,' David smiled, and linked his arm possessively through hers as they went downstairs to his car. 'I've booked at the Trattoo,' he continued. 'Though you look so lovely, I feel I should take you somewhere where we can dance. At least then I'd get to hold you.'

Lorna settled in the seat and smoothed her green silk skirt over her slim legs.

'You look almost your old self tonight,' he went on. 'I think you're finally putting on weight.'

She laughed. 'I'm afraid it's only this dress. That's why I wore it. The full skirt hides my bones.'

'Your bones are too good to hide.'

Used to his flattery, Lorna made no comment. David was fun to be with and always gave her a good time. Unlike Allan, he had decided not to specialise, and was now firmly entrenched in a fashionable and lucrative group practice in Kensington.

During dinner he kept her amused with a flow of anecdotes about his patients and their mainly imaginary ailments.

'My list seems to consist of middle-aged widows with too much money and too little to do. A visit from the doctor whiles away a pleasant half-hour of their day.'

'Don't you find it boring and unfulfilling?' Lorna asked critically.

'Only until I present them with my bill at the end of the month. Then I find their cheques *most* satisfying.' His grin softened the edge of the mercenary comment. 'We can't all be saintly and self-sacrificing like you.'

'What you really mean is that you think I'm a fool.'

'Truthfully, yes. You could be working in a private clinic like Ann for nearly twice your present pay. After all, what difference does it make whose life you're saving?'

'It makes a great difference to the Health Service,' Lorna replied. 'It's because so many doctors and nurses *are* thinking like *you* that it's in its present predicament.'

'Blame the Government, not the doctors and nurses. For years they've relied on us to do our so-called duty to our patients and to our calling, and because of it we've been given a rotten deal.'

'But don't you think we *do* have a duty?'

'Sure. But we also have a duty to ourselves.' He ran a square-fingered hand through his wavy hair. 'And that requires me to have a decent life and a substantial bank balance. Like Allan,' he reminded her. '*He* isn't working for the Health Service.'

Lorna blushed. 'He went to Kuwait to get the experience he wants. He'd have had to wait years for it in England.'

'I'm not knocking Allan,' David placated. 'I think he did the right thing. And so should you. Take this job Ann's found for you, and wallow in luxury for a bit.'

Lorna helped herself to another petit four and tried to disguise a yawn as she nibbled at it.

'You're tired,' David said instantly as he noticed it. 'I'll get the bill.'

A little later, drawing up outside her flat, he went to take her in his arms. But before he had time to do so Lorna had opened the door and was half out of it.

'What a hard-hearted wench you are,' he murmured, following her across the pavement. 'Won't you let me come in for a nightcap?'

'I'm terribly tired,' she excused herself.

'And terribly hard-hearted.'

'I'm sure you could find a soft-hearted girl-friend.'

'No doubt of it. But I'm a sucker for punishment.'

Blowing him a kiss, Lorna ran up the stone steps to the entrance of the converted Victorian mansion.

As she knew it would be, the flat was empty. Ann was on night duty. It was a good thing she had not let David come up with her. She pulled a face at her reflection as she passed the mirror in her bedroom. If only she could respond to him with more enthusiasm! But his kisses left her cold, and she was sure he was aware of it. Yet he seemed content to go on seeing her. Perhaps he hoped she would eventually overcome her inhibitions and succumb.

'My reluctant virgin,' he had once jokingly called her after a particularly energetic tussle, and how true it was. But she had always resisted casual affairs, determined that when she did give herself to a man, it would be because she loved him, and as far as she was concerned, love meant marriage.

The next afternoon, during her free period, Lorna went for her interview with Madam Rashid. She took special care to ensure that she did not look too pretty, for her looks had always been a

handicap in her chosen profession. Her employers
were invariably women, and most of them were
antagonistic towards anyone who possessed
glamour, seeming to believe that beauty and dedi-
cation to one's work could not possibly go together.

Sweeping back her thick blonde hair from her
oval face, she caught it in a loose bun at the nape
of her slender neck. Then she went to her wardrobe and surveyed her dresses, taking a couple out
and holding them up against herself. A navy one
was her final choice. She had bought it in a sale
at Harvey Nichols and immediately regretted it,
but it was perfect for this occasion and success-
fully screened the aura of sexuality that always
emanated from her; though it could not quite
hide the firm fullness of her breasts and her small
waist.

There was little she could do to disguise her
face. Her features were so well chiselled that even
the minimum amount of make-up enhanced them,
and ruefully aware of this, she used nothing but
moisturiser. Even so, her natural colouring gave
her a glow that caused a few male eyes to look
in her direction with appreciation as she went towards her car. But she refused to be downhearted.
She would have to be judged on merit. She was a
good nurse, with excellent references to prove it.

She was prompt to time when she arrived outside the marble portals of the luxurious block of
flats in Lowndes Square in which the Rashids
lived. A uniformed porter ignored her, but on
learning she was bound for the penthouse, ushered

her obsequiously to the lift, where she was
swished up to the tenth floor in seconds.

The doors did not slide open until she had given
her name into the answerphone that hung on the
wall of the lift, and when she did step out, a
uniformed maid was waiting to escort her through
the foyer into the main living-room. The entire
decor was cream and white; the walls in natural
raw silk and the units for drinks and china built in
and lacquered to match. Several Buffet paintings
and Topolski lithographs lined the walls, while
sepia tinted mirrors reflected the quiet-toned
elements. The only splashes of colour were the
exotically-patterned silk cushions scattered over
the tweed couches and armchairs.

Through the full-length windows she glimpsed
the terrace, and walking over to admire the view,
was astonished to find it was the size of an average suburban garden. It was laid out lavishly;
partly tiled in blue, with gold cherubs spouting
cascades of jewel-clear water into lily ponds, and
plants of every kind blooming in vivid profusion
from formal beds and elegant stone urns.

'Miss Masters?'

A soft voice made her spin round, and Lorna
saw Dana Rashid walking towards her. She was
an attractive girl, with a cloud of fluffy dark hair
that reached almost to her waist. Her face was
small, with neat features and huge, rather anxious
deep brown eyes. Her handclasp was firm and her
smile so welcoming that Lorna immediately felt
more relaxed.

Madam Rashid waved her into one of the cream

armchairs and seated herself opposite. 'Perhaps you would like to explain more fully how you heard about the position,' she began in faultless English. 'And also tell me something about yourself. My husband had hoped to interview you himself, but was called away on business and only gave me the briefest message before he left this morning.'

As concisely as she could, Lorna told her about Ann's phone call from the private clinic, and then produced her references.

'My husband was highly recommended to Miss Peters,' Madam Rashid said, glancing through them. 'But I'm sure you'll be a most suitable replacement. That is if you'll accept the position?'

Lorna looked into the dark brown eyes and felt a rapport between herself and this comely young woman. Yet she was still unwilling to commit herself.

'You'll find it far less tiring here than at the hospital,' the dark-haired girl went on anxiously. 'Amina is a very good baby, particularly at night. Would you like to see her?'

Following Dana Rashid down a wide, mirrored corridor past a seemingly endless succession of doors, Lorna came to the nursery, and they silently made their way over to the pink organdie crib which stood in the centre of the huge room. Sleeping soundly between hand-embroidered sheets was a plump, pretty baby, with a mop of tightly curled black hair. Even asleep, she looked the image of her mother.

'She's only four and a half months and already

cutting her first tooth,' came the proud boast. 'Isn't that rather early?'

Lorna nodded her agreement, although for the life of her she could not remember if this was true. Her child care training had been done during the early part of her course and she had not had much to do with young children since.

'The nurses' room adjoins this one,' Madam Rashid continued in a whisper, and beckoned Lorna to follow her into a room whose decor followed the same luxurious style as the rest of the apartment. 'Do say you'll come,' the younger girl continued. 'I know it sounds strange, but I feel a warmth towards you—as if I've known you before.'

Lorna hesitated, and then nodded. 'Would it be all right if I came here for a month on a trial basis? Then if either of us isn't happy. . . .'

'But we *will* be happy with each other. I know it. It will be so good to have someone of my own age with me.' Madam Rashid led the way back to the living-room, where a tea trolley awaited them. 'My husband is often out in the evenings, but as I am not allowed out on my own at night, it gets very lonely.'

'Don't you have any friends here?' asked Lorna.

'Yes, but they are all in the same position as myself. If anyone from home should see us out unaccompanied by our husbands . . .' She smiled as she saw Lorna's surprise. 'In Kuwait we still live in the past. We do not have the same freedom as you Westerners.'

'I had no idea you came from Kuwait,' Lorna

exclaimed with delight. 'I wonder if ... but no, that would be too much of a coincidence.'

Dana Rashid looked puzzled.

'I have a brother working there,' Lorna went on. 'He's head of gynaecology at the Saud Hospital.'

The younger girl's face turned pale and the cup she was holding dropped from her hand, spilling hot liquid over her dress and running down on to the white carpet. But she did not seem to notice and stared incomprehensibly at Lorna. Then she pulled herself together and dabbed at her dress with a wisp of lace handkerchief, at the same time pressing the bell for the maid, who hurried in, saw what had happened and rushed out to return with a wet cloth and a towel.

'It was stupid of me not to have realised who you were,' Dana Rashid said huskily. 'Allan told me you were a nurse. He spoke of you many times. It must be the will of Allah that has sent you here.'

Although the girl addressed Lorna directly, she murmured the words as if turning them over in her mind. But before Lorna could ask what she meant a heavily accented male voice spoke from the doorway.

'And what is the will of Allah today?'

'Hassan!' Dana Rashid gave a nervous start and followed this with a too bright smile, making a bold but not altogether successful effort to appear pleased. 'I didn't expect you home so early.'

A slim young man stepped forward into Lorna's view. Hassan Rashid was only a few inches taller than his wife, in spite of his elevated crocodile shoes. Immaculately attired in a light grey suit, he was much swarthier than she, which made him look far more Arabic. His handsome, rather boyish face sported a small, neatly trimmed beard and moustache, below which his full lips stretched into a wide smile as he was introduced to Lorna.

His small brown eyes rested on her with obvious admiration and his handclasp lingered longer than was necessary for politeness before he turned back to his wife.

Speaking rapidly in Arabic, he was obviously questioning her about the spilt tea. But she answered him in English, throwing Lorna an apologetic glance for his rudeness.

'The handle of the cup came off while I was adding the sugar,' the girl lied.

'I hope it doesn't stain,' he muttered crossly as the maid dabbed at the carpet with some water. 'I told you it was foolish to have white. But you always think you know best.' He turned to Lorna. 'My wife can be very stubborn and I need a great deal of patience to deal with her.'

'I am sure Miss Masters isn't interested in hearing about my faults,' Dana Rashid said gently, her composure regained.

'If she is to work here she will learn *all* about us soon enough,' he replied, his sharp brown eyes not moving from Lorna's face. 'I hope you have agreed to take Miss Peters' place?'

Lorna nodded, but knew that had she met this man first she would never have accepted the position. It was apparent that the Rashids were not on the best of terms, and she had no wish to become involved in domestic arguments. But it would have looked too obvious if she backed out now.

'We've agreed on a trial period,' she told him.

'Miss Masters is starting on Friday,' Dana interposed, and flashed Lorna a desperate look, as if pleading with her to agree.

'In that case,' the man said to Lorna, his voice smooth, 'I hope you will be happy here. We shall *both* do our best to ensure that you are.'

Lorna rose without replying. Hassan Rashid made her feel uncomfortable with his sly glances. 'I have to be going, Madam Rashid.'

'I'll walk with you to the lift,' the girl replied, clutching her sodden skirt in her hand. 'I must go and change anyway.'

With a polite nod towards Mr Rashid, Lorna followed her out.

'Thanks for not giving me away about the spilt tea,' she whispered when they were alone in the hall. 'I'll explain everything to you when we meet again.' She clasped Lorna's hands in her own. 'I think we will be good friends, no?'

'I'm sure of it,' Lorna replied, and felt a wave of sympathy for this seemingly unhappy girl. 'I'll see you on Friday, then?'

'You *are* sweet to come so soon, but my husband doesn't like me to go out and leave the baby with the maids and on Saturday we have been invited to dinner by friends who are returning to Kuwait. The wife was an old school friend of mine.'

'Were you educated here? Your English is perfect.'

Danà Rashid acknowledged the praise with a smile. 'I was at school in Switzerland, so my French and German are equally good. Khalid, my brother, doesn't approve of English boarding schools for girls. He says they either turn them out to be horsey, or rebellious bluestockings.'

Considering herself neither, despite a boarding-school education, Lorna felt a twinge of dislike for the unknown Khalid, with his high-handed assumptions.

'I can't say I agree with your brother,' she remarked drily.

The dark girl giggled. 'Nor do I. But he has very decisive opinions about women and likes to pigeonhole them.'

The lift doors opened and Lorna stepped in, keeping a smile on her face until the doors closed again and she was alone. Why hadn't Dana Rashid told her husband that she was Allan's sister? Surely that was the most natural thing for her to have done? For that matter, why hadn't Allan mentioned either of the Rashids in his letters home?

The explanation that came to Lorna's mind was one she did not care to think about. Surely sensible, dependable Allan would never jeopardise his career by having an affair with a married woman? Particularly in a country where adultery was considered a crime punishable by imprisonment and not so long ago death. But it was pointless to speculate about it. In a few days her questions would be answered by Dana Rashid.

Although it was a rush, Lorna managed to move in to Lowndes Square by Friday, and fortunately enough sublet her part of the flat without any delay. She also went to see Maggie Peters, the girl whom she had replaced at the Rashids. She was an attractive redhead, though she looked somewhat despondent as she lay in a small ward on the top floor of the clinic.

'Just my rotten luck,' she moaned. 'I took ages to find that set-up. There are plenty of good jobs going, but none with as many perks as this one. Perhaps you'll let me know when the job's free again?' She broke off to give Lorna a critical once-over. 'With your looks you shouldn't have to work there for long.'

Lorna was puzzled. 'I'm afraid I don't understand you.'

'Be nice to Hassan Rashid and his friends and you soon will,' came the retort. 'He has quite a reputation as a playboy. In fact it was through an ex-boy-friend of mine that I met him and he offered me the job.'

'Is that why you were taking it?' Lorna was staggered. 'To find yourself a rich boy-friend?'

'A rich husband preferably,' Maggie answered honestly. 'It's not difficult, because most Arabs find Western women very attractive. But you must hold out for marriage and not go to bed with them first. That's the way to catch them,' she advised. 'And even if they eventually take another wife it doesn't matter. You'll be left with enough money to ensure you won't need to empty bedpans again! A word of advice, though. Steer clear of sleeping with Hassan—he can be *very* persuasive. But if you play around with him his friends will all know and they'll expect the same perk. Then you can say goodbye to wedding bells!'

'I've no intention of playing around with anyone,' Lorna said abruptly.

'Then why did you take the job? Surely Ann explained the position?'

Lorna shook her head. 'I've been ill and I needed to find something that wasn't too strenuous. There was no other reason.'

A swift glance at Lorna's set expression made Maggie redden. But she carried off her embarrassment very well.

'Hassan will be in for a nasty surprise when he tries his luck on you,' she giggled defiantly. 'I'm sure he thinks I recommended you because you've got the same ideas as me.'

'The last thing I want is to have an affair with my employer or to marry any of his friends,' Lorna said coldly. 'I intend to spend *my* Arabian nights strictly alone.'

'More fool you! You'll just be wasting your opportunities.'

Lorna was relieved when she could finally get away from Maggie Peters. With a bit of luck that should be the last time she would have anything to do with her. The girl's suggestions had angered her, as no doubt Ann had known they would. That was why she had not told her the whole truth about the job. If she had, Lorna would never have gone for the interview. But at least Hassan

Rashid's oily familiarity had been explained. He obviously assumed that any friend of Maggie's would also be a friend of his. She only hoped his wife had no idea what was in his mind. But no, if she had, she would never have engaged her.

When David took her out to dinner that evening and she told him what had happened, he voiced his disapproval vociferously.

'You might not be interested in Mr Rashid or his friends, but that won't stop them from being interested in you. And they won't take no for an answer,' he added bluntly. 'You're a beautiful girl, and a temptation for any man. You should read some of the letters Allan's sent me from Kuwait. Fidelity is almost unknown there, and the way the men behave, especially when they're abroad, is unbelievable.'

Lorna forbore to answer that infidelity was hardly an invention of the Arabs. She was more concerned to find out if David knew of any connection between her brother and Dana Rashid. But she had to broach it discreetly.

'Allan's written to me too,' she replied. 'But I can promise you I won't be tempted by offers of air-conditioned palaces in Kuwait. Mock Tudor in Weybridge is more my style.' She spooned brown sugar into her coffee and kept her tone deliberately light. 'He keeps quiet about his own escapades, though. For a bachelor doctor he seems to lead a very celibate life.'

David threw her a sharp look that instantly told Lorna her brother *had* confided in him. And why not? Who better than his best friend, himself in the medical profession, so able to appreciate how important it was for a doctor to keep his good name?

'Don't worry about Allan,' said David. 'I can assure you he's not living like a monk.'

Knowing she was not going to get the answer she was looking for, Lorna stopped probing.

'Well, *I* intend to live like a nun at the Rashids',' she joked, 'so you needn't worry about me. If I could stand the onslaught of student doctors for six years, without losing my honour, I can assure you no marauding Arabs will stand a chance.'

But David refused to be consoled, and she realised from his genuine concern that he was fonder of her than she had believed. Once aware of this, she decided it was better not to see so much of him. If she could never love him it would be better not to monopolise his time. By continuing to see him, she was encouraging him to believe that something more meaningful might develop.

Because of this, she hedged when he asked to see her again.

'I haven't arranged my days off yet,' she excused herself.

'Let me know as soon as you do. I'm free any time—for you, that is,' he added meaningfully.

Lorna thought of this as she prepared for bed. If she did continue to see David, it would be easy to talk herself into believing she loved him. After all, they liked the same things and got on well together. Almost too well. But there was no magic—no spark of fire which she had always assumed would exist between herself and the man she would marry.

Was she romanticising to think this way, and would she be wiser to settle for companionship and understanding? She had reached the age when she would have to answer these questions. But for the moment she would put them out of her mind.

First things first; and the first thing was her job with the Rashids—and Allan's possible involvement with Dana Rashid.

CHAPTER TWO

'LORNA, I'd like you to meet my brother Khalid.'

With a start, Lorna looked up from feeding the baby her evening bottle and saw a tall figure in the shadow of the nursery doorway.

'Khalid,' Dana continued, 'this is Lorna, my angel in disguise.'

'I'm surprised to find she isn't wearing a halo. Your letters have done nothing but sing her praises for the past three months.'

Stung by the sarcastic tones, Lorna tried to mask her annoyance, and hoped she had also masked her surprise at finding the man so unlike his sister. He was exceptionally tall, and though

his hair was as thick and as sleekly black as any
Arab sheikh, the eyes that looked down to meet
her own were as brilliantly blue as a Viking war-
rior—and contained just about as much warmth.

Khalid al Hashib looked to be in his early thirties. He was wearing an impeccably cut navy suit
and his white shirt emphasised the golden glow of
his skin. His eyebrows were as black as his hair,
and a firm, straight nose above a wide sensuous
mouth divided a face that was not only handsome,
but full of character. There was more than a hint
of obstinacy in the determined thrust of his square
jaw, but it was the eyes that fascinated: as well as
being piercingly intense, they were an impossible
colour for an Arab.

Lorna's reaction was not lost on Dana, who regarded her with barely concealed amusement. Nor
was it lost on her brother.

'I see Dana didn't tell you I am only her half-
brother and that my mother was English? It's a
trick she enjoyed playing on her school friends
when she invited them home for the holidays,
but I assumed she had outgrown such childish-
ness.'

'I wasn't being childish this time,' his sister
protested halfheartedly, and turned to Lorna.
'Khalid's mother was my father's first wife, and
when they divorced——'

'Spare the explanation till I've gone,' he interrupted coldly, and stepped forward to look at his
niece who was drowsily sucking at her bottle.
'She looks like you, Dana, when you were her
age.' His voice was mellifluous now, even beau-

tiful, with dark velvety tones, and he chuckled indulgently as the baby gave him a windy, lopsided smile.

'How can you possibly remember?' his sister asked. 'You were only nine.'

'You were such a beautiful baby, how could I forget?' he answered teasingly, and took a step backwards to put his arm affectionately around her shoulders, as if wishing to atone for his earlier ill-humour. 'May I hold Amina when she's finished her supper?'

He addressed the question to Lorna, his tone cool again, and equally coolly he eyed her, making no effort to hide the fact that he was not impressed with what he saw.

For the first time since she had started to work for the Rashids, Lorna wished she had not made her appearance so unattractive. But warned by what Maggie Peters had said, she had gone further than she had done for her first interview, seeing it as the one sure way to prevent unwanted advances.

She wore no make-up and scraped her hair under a flat nurse's cap—the least flattering she could find. Her figure was hidden beneath a calf-length starched white dress which, for good measure, she did not belt, knowing gleefully that it made her look shapeless. Yet seeing the lack of interest in those bright blue eyes she knew an unexpected pang. It would have given her pleasure if this imperious-looking man *had* made an advance which she could rebuff.

Even before meeting him she had disliked the

picture of him which Dana had painted and, in his presence, it was confirmed. Not only was he domineering, but he was also disdainful, and she had the distinct impression that he was annoyed that a stranger had so quickly gained the affection of his sister.

Yet in spite of her antipathy towards him she found herself aware of the strength he exuded, and to hide her confusion at this mixed reaction she busied herself with the baby; placing the empty bottle on the nursery trolley and laying the child over her shoulders to pat her back until she burped. Only then did she stand up and hand Amina over to her uncle.

At five feet six Lorna was fairly tall, but she felt almost short as she reached up towards him. His height alone gave away his mixed birth, because in all the months she had been working here, no Arab had towered above her as this man did.

He held the baby firmly in the crook of his arm, showing none of the awkwardness that Amina's own father displayed.

'She's heavier than she looks,' he commented after a few minutes of indulgent admiration.

'Weaning her early hasn't done her any harm,' Dana replied. 'Mother kept telephoning me with all sorts of old-fashioned notions about the folly of putting her on the bottle so early, and if it hadn't been for Lorna, I'd still be breast-feeding.'

'From your letters to me, I gather your nanny thinks most of our ways old-fashioned.' He looked at Lorna, a hint of warning in his eyes. 'You would be wise to remember that Western ideas are not applicable to our women. To persuade my sister otherwise is dangerous.'

'I've never tried to influence your sister, Mr al Hashib,' Lorna replied stiffly. 'I just give my opinion when it's asked for. Being a Westerner doesn't come into it. As far as I'm concerned, as members of the same sex we presumably have the same feelings.'

'On the contrary. A different culture leads to different feelings—regardless of your sex being the same.' His mouth was tight with anger, making it clear that he did not like to have his beliefs questioned. 'Bearing that in mind, it would be better if you kept your opinions to yourself.'

'Khalid!' Dana was clearly shocked by her brother's bluntness, and as if he realised it, he gave her a half-smile.

'I think it's best for me to say what I feel.' His voice was gentle this time. 'No doubt your nurse, like most Englishwomen of her class, prefers to have the truth.'

'I'm a great believer in the truth,' Lorna said without expression. 'So perhaps you will forgive me if I do not agree with the comment you made a moment ago. No matter how different the cultures, women share a common bond in their feeling capacity, and men share a common bond in their lack of understanding of women.'

There was a short silence before Khalid al Hashib spoke again.

'Those are fighting words.'

'I don't wish to fight with you—sir.'

'I'm glad to hear it. I've never lost a battle yet.'
The look he gave her was cold and hard before he
turned to his sister. 'I'll have a bath and a change
of clothes,' he said abruptly, and handed his niece
back to Lorna.

His long brown fingers lightly brushed her arm,
and she was annoyed that she could not suppress
the tingle of excitement his touch aroused. Because of this she remained bent over the cot until
he and Dana had left the room. Only then did she
tidy the nursery and go into her bedroom.

Unsure of the arrangements for this evening,
Lorna did not change immediately. Normally she
dined with Dana—unless there were guests—for
Hassan was rarely home for dinner. But Khalid's
arrival might change things, for he gave the impression that he saw her as a subordinate—and
one with whom one did not partake salt. He
would have liked her even less had he known of
his sister's relationship with Allan.

As always when she thought of her brother and
Dana, Lorna knew a deep sense of disquiet. Dana
had told her the truth about their relationship
within a week of her coming to the flat, and
though it had served to bring the two of them
closer together, it had also added to Lorna's fears.

Dana had met Allan some time after her marriage to Hassan, who was her cousin. Their be-
trothal had been arranged between the two families when they were schoolchildren. It was a
marriage Dana had not wanted and she had
pleaded with Khalid to allow her the freedom of
choice that a Western education had taught her

to see as her right. But he had refused. Her Westernisation was expected to come to a halt after the completion of her education, and she was ordered to comply with the wishes of her family in the traditional manner.

As head of the household since the death of their father in a plane crash, Khalid's word was law, and to have disobeyed him would have made Dana a social outcast. As much as he loved his sister, Khalid was not prepared to disregard his father's wishes, and it would have taken a stronger-willed girl than the eighteen-year-old Dana to have defied him. Besides, she had no money of her own and was only educated to spend it, not earn any.

At least Hassan was young, single and good-looking, whereas many of her friends were forced into marriages with much older men who sometimes had other wives. Therefore she had accepted the inevitable and had determined to make the best of things. Arranged marriages had been a way of life for her people for centuries, and it had worked out quite happily for others, including her own parents, so perhaps it would for her.

Unfortunately Hassan made no effort to make the marriage work, and regarded his entry into the fabulously wealthy al Hashib family as licence to indulge himself without financial restraint. He saw Dana's role as that of the acquiescent mother of his children, while he himself continued his role as a playboy.

'Naturally I was a virgin when we married,' Dana had explained somewhat shyly to Lorna.

'But I knew the facts of life, which is more than I can say for many of my friends. I knew that sex should be enjoyable for me as well as for him. But he refused to see my point of view. He had the same antiquated ideas as most of our men—that a wife is a man's most precious possession, and therefore to make love to her, as opposed to making her pregnant, would dishonour her.'

'Dishonour her?' Lorna had questioned.

'Yes. Our men believe they should only *take* pleasure from their wives—not give it. That is why a lot of them have Western women. Not to marry, of course, purely for enjoyment.'

'Of course,' Lorna had said dryly, restraining her abhorrence of such antiquated thinking.

'When I was married for a year I begged my brother to let me get a divorce,' Dana continued. 'But he wouldn't hear of it. He said it was my duty to accept whatever my husband did. He told me to have a child and said it would occupy me and perhaps bring Hassan to heel, especially if I gave him a son.'

In the event it had not worked. Dana had had a miscarriage and Hassan had continued on his merry way. Increasingly unhappy, Dana obtained her husband's permission to do voluntary work in the women's wards at the Saud hospital. It was there that she had met Allan. But the friendship did not deepen until six months later, by which time she was already pregnant again.

She pleaded with Allan to leave Kuwait with her after the baby was born, and had been prepared to relinquish her maternal rights if he would

agree. But Allan had known that once Dana held
her child in her arms she would not wish to abandon it, and he had been proved right. Realising
Hassan would never let her take Amina away
with her, she and Allan had agreed to stop seeing
each other, and they had both been relieved when
Khalid said he wanted Hassan to live in London
and manage the family's business interests there.

'I jumped at the chance,' Dana had told Lorna,
'because I knew I would never forget Allan if we
were living in the same city. I believed that if we
were thousands of miles apart I would stop wanting him, but I miss him more than ever.'

Lorna had sought for words of comfort, but
they all seemed too banal for her to utter, and she
had satisfied herself with trying to look as sympathetic as she could. Yet with all honesty she was
glad Dana was now living in England. For Allan to
have an affair with a married Kuwaiti woman
would spell disaster for him.

'Do you think it wrong of me to love your
brother?' Dana had asked unexpectedly.

'Not wrong,' Lorna had said quickly. 'But unwise. No one can help falling in love. But you
should make every effort to forget him.'

'I can't! Until Allan came into my life I never
understood what it was to love a man with all my
heart, and now we have to spend the rest of our
lives apart. By the time Amina is grown up and I
feel free to leave her, Allan will have found someone else.'

Lorna had not replied. To her way of thinking it
was not only Dana's love for her daughter which

made marriage to Allan impossible, but the fact that he was a doctor and head of the Gynaecology Department of the hospital when he had met Dana. Such a fact—even though he had not been her own personal doctor—was enough to discredit him in the eyes of the British Medical Association. She knew Dana would not see things this way and wondered if fate had brought her into the girl's life in order to make sure that she continued to keep out of Allan's—at least until he was safely married to someone else.

Now that she had met Khalid, Lorna was even more afraid for her brother. Were Khalid to suspect how his sister felt, he would have no compunction in destroying Allan.

It was incredible to think that Khalid, a man of obvious education—he had graduated with honours from Oxford—could so adhere to the past and uphold old-fashioned and harsh traditions. Since taking over the family business on his father's death, he had built it into a multi-national combine. In *that* respect at least, he lived very much in the present.

Lorna wondered if he applied the same anti-quated standards to himself and would maintain an unhappy marriage just because it was the custom. She knew he was still single and she pitied the wife he would eventually choose. She would have to be subservient and unthinking, prepared to regard him as her master, and to subjugate herself to his every desire. No doubt she would also be kept in purdah behind the walls of his air-conditioned harem!

It was easy to picture him in the role of an Eastern potentate, and she wondered about his mother, whose influence on him had evidently been nil.

'Not changed yet?' Dana's lilting voice interrupted Lorna's reverie. 'Dinner is in half an hour and I want you to have a drink with us first and get acquainted with Khalid before Hassan comes back. Once the two men get together they'll discuss business for the rest of the evening.'

Lorna was certain Khalid had no desire to get acquainted with *her*, but did not voice this opinion to Dana.

'I wasn't sure if you would want me to dine with you,' she said.

'Of course I do, though I wish you wouldn't make yourself look so frumpish. When you came here the first time you looked much better.'

'I'm here as Amina's nurse, and I should dress accordingly.'

Dana looked as if she were going to disagree, then she thought better of it. 'At least put on a bit of make-up. Amina's fast asleep and she'll never know!'

It was a temptation for Lorna to do as she was told, but she resisted it and merely took off her cap.

Dana looked disappointed when she entered the lounge a short while later, still dressed in her uniform. But she made no comment, only raising one eyebrow quizzically.

Khalid, who had been seated in an armchair sipping a whisky, stood up politely as she entered and gave her a faint smile. He appeared to be more relaxed, and had changed into another dark suit of the same impeccable cut. But his shirt was light blue and emphasised the colour of his eyes. Her traitorous pulse quickened as he caught her gaze and held it, and she was relieved to seat herself next to Dana and avert her eyes, while he busied himself at the bar after enquiring what she would like to drink.

'Dana told me your brother works at the Saud hospital,' he said, handing her a dry Martini.

His remark was so unexpected that she had to fight to control the trembling of her hand. What on earth had possessed Dana to tell her brother about Allan? But then she realised she was being foolish. No one in Dana's family knew that the girl loved Allan, and to have hidden Lorna's relationship with him would have looked suspicious.

'Yes,' she answered as casually as she could. 'Allan's been there for a couple of years. I gather from his letters that he's very happy, although he finds the climate unpleasant.'

'Don't we all! That's why those of us who can spend their summers abroad. There's a mass exodus in April that nicely coincides with the rise in house and flat prices in London and the Home Counties.'

Lorna could not suppress a smile at his remark. 'Are the winters much better? Allan says the nights are cold and the days windy.'

'At least they're predictable—unlike your winters here—or your summers, for that matter.'

He returned to his chair, walking with an easy

grace that made her wonder what he would look like in Arab robes. 'Have you never thought of going to visit your brother, Miss Masters? I'm sure you would find our country most interesting.'

'I'm sure I would,' Lorna agreed. 'I had intended going this year, but I wasn't well, and I had to cancel it.'

'Ah yes,' he murmured. 'Dana mentioned it in one of her letters. Are you in good health now? If you're looking after a baby. . . .'

'I'm perfectly all right now,' Lorna interposed hurriedly, wondering if he were looking for a way to get rid of her. 'Working for your sister is like a holiday compared with my job at the hospital.'

'When do you intend returning?' he asked.

'I've managed to persuade Lorna to stay on for another couple of months,' Dana cut in. 'But please don't talk about her leaving me. I———'

'Who's leaving you, my pet?' The oily smooth voice of Dana's husband came floating across the room as he flung his briefcase down on a chair and came forward to peck her on the cheek before greeting his brother-in-law.

'We were talking about Lorna,' his wife replied.

Hassan's dark face clouded. 'I have already offered her more money to stay with us for a year. What else can I do?'

'My wishing to leave has nothing to do with money,' Lorna was quick to point out. 'But I'm a hospital nurse and I want to get back to that kind of work. In any case, you pay me more than enough already.'

'Then perhaps your fondness for my wife will persuade you to stay.'

Lorna did not reply. She had already had this conversation with Hassan and knew it was useless to go on arguing. He was a spoiled man who was too used to having his own way. Since he had learned she intended to leave, he had bombarded her with inducements to make her change her mind—not so much for Dana's sake, but for his own. It suited him to have her here because Dana had been much easier to live with since her arrival, and their quarrelling had almost ceased. Indifference had taken its place, and Dana no longer objected when he spent his nights at the casinos or with women. With Lorna as a companion, her hours were always whiled away pleasantly, and she was no longer lonely.

'I don't understand why you prefer to slave in a hospital when you can remain here,' Hassan commented into the silence. 'Or do you find the lack of male company irksome?'

Avoiding Hassan's eyes, Lorna turned her head and saw Khalid's blue ones. They held amusement and she knew he was wondering how any man would want to waste time in the company of such a dowdy-looking girl. She moved in her chair and her starched dress, a size too big, rustled forbiddingly.

'Neither men nor money has anything to do with Lorna's decision.' Dana glanced reprovingly at her husband before looking at her brother. 'Lorna doesn't find looking after Amina sufficiently occupying.'

'Then you should give her some more children to look after,' said Khalid. 'Having children and taking care of them is a natural occupation for all women.'

'It's not the only role for us to play,' Lorna intervened coldly. 'Our genes have made us child-bearers, but we don't have to devote our entire lives to it. We aren't all born to be earth-mothers, you know.'

'It is a woman's main function.'

With an effort, Lorna held on to her temper. 'It would be a waste of my training if I were to give up work completely when I have children.'

'Will you allow someone else to bring them up and abdicate your responsibilities?' Khalid enquired. 'I am not surprised the Western world is full of juvenile delinquents. *We* believe a woman's place is in the home and no one encourages her to feel guilty for wishing to remain there. Western society has made the female go against her natural instincts and forced her to feel inferior should she wish to play a purely domestic role.' He gave a condescending smile. 'In fact, it is the one role that suits her best.'

Lorna longed to slap him. It was incredible that an educated man should think in this way, and even though there was an element of truth in what he said, his insistence that everyone should feel the same destroyed the force of his argument.

'Even women who enjoy domesticity often want to play another role too,' she said. 'Feminine intellect is no different from that of the male.'

Lorna caught Dana's eye and detected both caution and admiration. 'Although you think we're cow-like creatures with no minds of their own,' she continued, 'I——'

'I know what *you* think,' Khalid cut in. 'But since we've just met, aren't you being presumptuous in assuming you know what *I* think?'

'It isn't hard to guess what's in your mind,' his sister interpolated. 'You make it very clear the way you regard women. But I suggest we change the subject and go in for dinner.'

Considering the evening's inauspicious beginning, the meal passed off well. Lorna was seated opposite Khalid and often caught him staring thoughtfully at her, as if trying to sum her up, and no doubt pigeonhole her too. He had the disconcerting habit of not averting his gaze when it met her own, and she was always the first to turn away.

In spite of her antipathy towards him she found him an interesting raconteur, and could not help joining in the laughter that his tales provoked. He gossiped amusingly about friends and family, and told anecdotes about his holidays, mentioning the names of the people who had accompanied him.

Most of them were also known to Dana and Hassan and appeared to be mainly Western business friends. If he had had a girl-friend with him, he did not mention her. Perhaps in Kuwaiti society it was not considered 'good form' to discuss one's affairs in front of other females.

As a maid cleared away their coffee cups and

placed a bottle of cognac and two brandy balloons on the glass-topped table, Dana rose and signalled Lorna to follow her.

'I'm sure the men are dying to talk business,' she said.

Neither of them bothered to deny it, and as Hassan reached for the bottle, Khalid stood up and opened the door for them. Lorna met his gaze and he made no effort to hide his amusement.

'Aren't you used to having the door opened for you, in your liberated society, Nurse?'

With a shake of her head she disclaimed the question, but answered it with another of her own.

'I didn't think Arab men observed the niceties of chivalry, *sir*.'

'We are taught to protect our women,' he replied.

'As second class citizens I'm sure they need it.'

The momentary narrowing of his eyes was his only concession to anger, but he was quick to hide it and made no comment, merely giving her a smile that disclosed perfectly formed white teeth. It was almost as if he were telling her that he knew he was irresistible and would eventually win her over.

Lorna walked slowly down the corridor, aware of his eyes burning into her back. She resisted the urge to run and it was with a feeling of relief that she heard the dining-room door shut behind her. She already regretted having been so frank with him. It had been tantamount to rudeness, and as he was the brother of her employer, she should have held her tongue.

Yet when she said as much to Dana, the girl disagreed.

'It will do Khalid good to have a woman give him an argument. Even though he spends so much of his time in the West, he isn't used to someone like you. The wives of his business friends are careful not to disagree with him, and his girl-friends treat him as if he's a god.'

Lorna's expression spoke volumes and Dana giggled. 'His latest girl-friend is just like all the rest—high in beauty and low in brains.'

'Doesn't he find them boring?' asked Lorna.

'Not if they're good in bed. He gets his mental stimulus from his men friends.'

'How long has his present affair lasted?'

'Almost a year—which is something of a record.'

'Do you think he'll marry her?'

'Khalid would never marry a Westerner,' said Dana, and then looked embarrassed. 'I'm sorry, Lorna. I——'

'You haven't offended me,' Lorna smiled. 'What you mean is that your brother thinks Western women are suitable for bedding, not wedding.'

Dana nodded. 'Khalid will apply the same rules to himself as he applied to me.' Her voice lowered. 'I only hope he will be happier.'

'I can't see him allowing a woman to make him unhappy. He's too full of his own importance to allow anyone else to be important to him.'

Dana chuckled. 'I can see *you* weren't bowled over by him! But I can assure you that when you get to know him better you will like him.'

Lorna doubted this, but did not say so. 'Why didn't you tell me he was only your half-brother?' she asked.

'Because I never think of him that way. He is so much like our father that I sometimes feel as if Father is living again through Khalid.'

'But your brother is half English.'

'It is a half he prefers to forget.'

Dana kicked off her high-heeled sandals and curled her feet under the soft tweed cushion on the settee. In a scarlet kaftan that emphasised her glossy black hair she presented such a lovely and exotic picture that Lorna could understand why Allan had found her so desirable. But thank heavens he had managed not to lose control of himself.

She switched her thoughts back to Khalid. 'Considering his mother was English, I'm surprised he's so adamant about not marrying a Westerner.'

'You wouldn't think so if you knew the whole story.'

Lorna wished she could, but refused to admit it, and she was delighted when Dana proceeded to recount it.

Khalid's father Achmed had been studying law at Oxford when he had met and married the girl who had become his first wife. To begin with the marriage had been happy. Khalid was born in England, but when he was a year old, Achmed had been ordered to return to Kuwait by his own father, whose health was failing. It was then that the trouble began.

'Khalid's mother refused to leave England,' Dana said, 'and for the next few years our father commuted. But of course he was very unhappy and eventually his family persuaded him to take another wife—the cousin to whom he had originally been betrothed. They were married according to Moslem law, which as you know permits a man to have more than one wife.'

'Did Khalid's mother accept that?'

Dana shook her head. 'It caused the final rift. She quarrelled bitterly with our father and refused to have anything more to do with him. By this time she was running a very successful decorating business and that became her only love.'

'What happened to Khalid?' asked Lorna.

'She sent him to Kuwait. She had no time for him and wouldn't even have him to stay with her for the holidays. That's why he has a hang-up about Western career women.'

'His mother certainly sounds a horror,' Lorna agreed. 'But he shouldn't judge all of us by the same yardstick.'

'You should tell him that! Then sit back and wait for the explosion.'

Lorna could well imagine it. 'Where's his mother now?'

'In New York. Khalid never sees her, but I've kept up with her career through the decorator magazines. She's top in her field, so she's often quoted and photographed.' Dana stared thoughtfully at Lorna. 'Don't judge my brother too harshly. At heart he is good and kind.'

'By his own standards, perhaps.'

'They are the standards of our race. That is something you should try to understand.'

'Do you understand them?' Lorna asked. 'If you were a Westerner you wouldn't be forced to remain with a man you don't love. You wouldn't have had to marry him in the first place.'

She bit back the rest of what she wanted to say, knowing she dared not encourage Dana to rebel. If she did, it might rebound on Allan.

Almost as if she guessed what Lorna was thinking, Dana's eyes filled with tears. 'No matter what differences there are between one race and another, they become unimportant when love steps in. Until I met your brother I had forced myself to accept Khalid's wishes for me to remain with Hassan. But once I knew the meaning of true love I would have given up everything for Allan— everything except my baby. Yet sometimes the thought of living like this for the rest of my life is more than I can bear. If only Khalid would agree to help me I *know* he could persuade Hassan to divorce me and let me keep Amina.'

'But he won't help you,' Lorna stated flatly. 'He's made that quite clear.'

Dana gave a deep sigh. 'Khalid doesn't believe in love. Until he knows for himself how it can tear at the heart. . . .'

'I doubt if he ever will,' Lorna replied, and then deliberately changed the subject, so that by the time the two men came into the room they were composedly talking about clothes.

But as she lay in bed later that night, Lorna's thoughts again turned to Khalid and his country. With all the wealth Kuwait had, it seemed reasonable to suppose that as it developed technically it would also develop intellectually, and would allow its women the same progress. But this might take another twenty years, and girls like Dana and probably Amina too, would have to content themselves with a restricted existence. They would be cosseted like dolls and treated as if they had the same sense. She thought of the life Dana had to lead and felt a great deal of sympathy for Khalid's British mother who, had she gone to live in her husband's country, would never have been allowed to dine in a public place or be seen in mixed company.

Lorna tried to envisage what her own life would have been like had she been born a Kuwaiti. From cradle to grave she would have been dominated and answerable to father, brother or husband. It was enough to make her hackles rise. With all its faults, England was not such a bad place to live after all.

CHAPTER THREE

FOR the next few days Lorna only saw Khalid during his brief visits to the nursery, where he would gaze upon his niece with an unusually tender expression. He did not speak to Lorna, except for a polite greeting, and she knew he had relegated her to the position of servant.

On the fourth evening of his visit his sister was giving a dinner party for him, and at Dana's request Lorna arranged the flowers for it. She was in the middle of doing the centrepiece for the dining-room when the girl sought her out again.

'I've just had a call from Lady Hartly. Her daughter's ill and can't make it this evening, which means we're a woman short.' She plucked petulantly at the petals of an orange chrysanthemum. 'Where can I possibly find another attractive girl at such short notice?'

Lorna looked up from the silver rose bowl she had been working on.

'Why not ask your brother? I'm sure he's got a long list.'

'I've a much better idea,' Dana replied, her brown eyes sparkling. 'Why don't you help out? You're by far the prettiest girl I know—or at least you are when you take off that dreadful uniform.'

'How can you be so sure?' Lorna asked, averting her face.

'Because I saw you in a dressing-gown one night when Amina woke up with a fever and we both went in to see her. I don't know why you're pretending to be plain, but I think you're mad.'

'Most women employers prefer it.'

'Oh.' Dana's response was telling. Then she shrugged. 'Well, I don't object. I'd love you to look your normal self and I'd adore to see Khalid's face when he discovers what you really look like.'

Lorna shook her head. 'I still don't think he'd appreciate having to make polite conversation with your nanny all evening.'

'Don't be so stuffy! He knows I regard you as my friend. Anyway, once you're out of that starchy dress he'll see you as a woman—and nothing else.'

'I don't think I like that either.'

Dana giggled like a schoolgirl, making Lorna realise that for all her outward sophistication, she was very young. It seemed mean not to help her out. Besides, it *would* be fun to see Khalid's face when she walked into the room in all her natural glory.

'Very well,' she said. 'I'll stand in for your sick guest.'

As soon as Lorna had settled Amina for the night, she went to her room to change. The first thing to do was to discard her severe hair-style, and she washed her hair and set it in Carmen rollers while she had a bath. After riffling through her wardrobe she selected a simple but expensive pleated chiffon dress which had been a birthday present from her parents. The hyacinth blue colour made her skin seem fairer, while the narrow shoulder straps that held up the tightly fitting bodice showed off her creamy shoulders and graceful neck. Set free from its pins her hair glinted like sun-kissed corn, and she let it fall in loose waves from a centre parting.

'You look like a golden-haired Madonna,' David had said when he had first seen her in this dress, and she wondered if Khalid al Hashib would think so too.

I don't give a damn what he thinks, she thought irritably. I'm only dressing up tonight to please Dana.

Nevertheless she felt decidedly nervous as she made her way into the lounge, her skirts swaying around her slender legs.

She was not the first one there. The family were already gathered and on their first drink. Dana looked every inch the wife of a millionaire in her emerald silk St Laurent, with dazzling jewels to match, while the two men wore dinner jackets—Hassan's a conventional black and Khalid's of wine velvet. It gave a warm glow to his skin and made his hair shine like black satin. It was impossible not to compare him favourably with his brother-in-law, for he stood head and shoulders above him in both senses of the word.

At her entry both men stood up, and both looked at her enquiringly, as if they did not know who she was. It was Khalid who guessed first, and

his astonishment was so profound that Lorna
wanted to laugh in his face.

'Well, well,' he drawled. 'So the duck has become a swan! I had a feeling your starched uniform was hiding something more than skinny legs
and a flat chest. But tell me, why have you hidden
your charms until now?'

'Amina doesn't mind a starchy uniform,' Lorna
said composedly. 'And I'm here to be in charge of
her.'

'But this evening I hope you'll be taking charge
of me, Lorna? I may call you that? I refuse to call
you Nanny.'

She shrugged, aware of him watching her. He
was standing so close that his breath stirred her
hair, and she took a step away from him.

'You must call me Khalid,' he murmured softly.
'It is much better than referring to me as Dana's
tyrannical brother. I hope I can convince you I
am nowhere near as hard-hearted as you imagine
—at least where beautiful women are concerned.'

'What are you saying to make Lorna blush?'
Hassan asked, his sharp eyes missing nothing. 'I've
never succeeded in doing so.'

Before Khalid could reply the first guests were
announced, and Lorna did not have a chance to
speak to him again.

A middle-aged American monopolised her for
most of the time, while the other men eyed him
with envy at having cornered the prettiest girl in
the room. All the couples were middle-aged, the
wives expensively well dressed and with little to
talk about except the social scene, so that she was

relieved when dinner was finally served and she found herself seated next to Khalid.

Although she was used to the excellent food served in the Rashid household, tonight Marcel, the French chef, had excelled himself. Hassan had enticed him away from one of Paris' finest restaurants, and he now travelled all over the world with him. Each course he presented was a masterpiece, not only a joy to taste but also to see. Lobster soufflé was followed by iced vichyssoise, then a golden boeuf en croute, the pastry lined with foie gras. For dessert there were crêpes suzettes, flambéd by Marcel, complete with white chef's hat, at the table. Only Dom Perignon champagne was served, and it flowed as generously as if it were water.

Lorna tried to do justice to the food, but found it impossible with Khalid beside her. Whether it was the champagne that had heightened her senses she did not know, but she was ultra-conscious of each movement he made, particularly when he turned and his leg inadvertently touched hers.

'You've hardly eaten a thing,' he remarked as one of the servants cleared away her barely touched dessert. 'Has the old bore next to you taken away your appetite?'

'With actions rather than words,' Lorna murmured.

'Sorry about that. But he specifically asked to sit next to the loveliest girl in the room, and since he's chairman of the bank that finances our oil tankers, I thought I'd better oblige.' His voice was serious, but there was a twinkle in his eyes.

'I thought you were rich enough to finance your own oil tankers,' she commented dryly.

'We are. But I prefer to use other people's cash.'

'How interesting that your dislike of Western ways doesn't apply to Western money.'

'I never confuse business with pleasure,' he said coldly. 'In any event, the remark you have made is more applicable to your people than to mine.' Seeing her puzzlement he said smoothly: 'Your countrymen may profess to despise our old-fashioned traditions, yet they are willing to do anything to benefit from our new-fashioned wealth.'

Because his comment was justified, she made no attempt to disagree with him.

'Have you nothing to say?' he asked, dark brows raised.

'I cannot argue against the truth, Mr al Hashib.'

'Indeed? I never thought I'd hear you say that. Thank you, Lorna. But you would sound more friendly if you called me Khalid, as I asked.'

'I'm sorry, but it's hard for me to think of you that way. I still see you as. . . .' Embarrassed by what she had been about to say, she let her voice trail away.

But he was not going to let her off and he leaned closer. A lock of silky dark hair fell over his forehead and he smoothed it back with long brown fingers.

'As an Eastern potentate?' he said. 'I can see you still haven't forgiven me for my attitude to women.'

'Why should that surprise you?'

'Because I didn't mean half of what I said.'

'Even the half you *did* mean is intolerable!'

He flung back his head and laughed. 'You have a sharp tongue, Lorna. I like it.'

'I'm so pleased,' she said sarcastically.

'Good. That makes two of us.'

Sharp-tongued or not, she could not think of a sufficiently cutting reply and concentrated on peeling a peach.

'It has the same bloom as your skin,' Khalid said in her ear.

'What an original compliment,' she said, poker-faced. 'You should write advertising copy. You'd make a fortune.'

'I've already made a fortune,' he said complacently.

'I was under the impression your grandfather made it.'

'Only the first million—which was pretty good going considering his office was the back of a camel and his horizons were limited by sand.'

'But think what lay beneath that sand.'

'I do,' he replied, and was unexpectedly serious. 'Oil was a gift from Allah and we must use its benefits wisely.'

Lorna thought of the extravagances of the Arabs whose names figured in the gossip columns, and wondered how this man would defend them.

'You have a very expressive face, Lorna. And I agree with you that many of my fellow-countrymen don't wear their wealth in a way I admire.'

'How do you spend yours?' she asked.

'By creating work and jobs for my people. Admittedly the salary I allow myself is considered phenomenal by the standards of the average man, but I assure you it is a minimal amount compared with what I invest in industry and commerce.'

He spoke with such seriousness that she could not accuse him of conceit, and knew that on his own terms he was indeed an admirable man. Yet she still had to provoke him, though she did not know why.

'You don't believe in false modesty, do you, Khalid?'

'I leave that to the British.' There was a mocking glint in his eyes which intensified their blueness.

'You're half British too,' she said, and saw his face harden.

'I prefer to remember my father's blood.'

'That's a ridiculous thing to say!'

He was suddenly so still that she knew she had overstepped the mark.

'I—I'm sorry,' she stumbled. 'I had no right to——'

'Don't worry about it,' he said thinly. 'Women always let their tongues run away with them. That is why one should never take them seriously.'

Anger swamped her, but she swallowed it back, glad when they were able to return to the lounge for coffee.

Somewhat to her chagrin, Khalid excused himself from her side and moved to talk to another of the guests; nor did he return to her side when his conversation was over. Instead he joined a group of men and was soon so immersed that she knew he had totally forgotten her. But that was the way he regarded women : as objects of passion and light entertainment, to be placed on a shelf when something more serious was at hand.

However she did not lack companionship, though the man who offered it was not to her taste, and she was relieved when his wife signalled him that it was time to depart. This heralded everyone else's leavetaking, and Khalid joined his sister and brother-in-law in the hall as they said goodbye. Overtly Lorna studied him, noticing how self-possessed he seemed, his bearing firm and authoritative.

'I think the evening was a great success,' Hassan remarked with satisfaction as the family returned to the lounge.

'And so was Lorna,' Khalid added. 'She was the delight of all the men and the envy of all the women.'

'I noticed Mrs Smythe-Morton giving her a few odd looks,' Dana agreed, and turned to Lorna. 'What was she saying to you?'

'She seemed put out to discover I was your nanny. In an upper-crust English household this sort of fraternisation is frowned upon.'

'We're much more democratic in Kuwait,' Dana commented.

'I can't agree with that,' Khalid contradicted. 'It's only because Lorna is English that we treat her differently. We wouldn't ask our servants at home to join us for dinner.'

Hassan yawned loudly, obviously bored by the conversation. 'I'm going to bed.' He looked at Dana and dutifully she stood up. 'I'll be leaving at nine tomorrow,' Hassan informed his brother-in-law. 'Will you be coming to the office with me or shall I send the car back for you later?'

'I'll see how I feel in the morning.'

'You should feel wonderful,' Hassan chuckled, and looked so sly that Lorna wondered if they had pulled off some business coup this evening.

As the door closed behind him and Dana, she stood up. 'I'll say goodnight too. Amina wakes up at seven no matter what time *I* go to bed.'

'Don't leave yet.' Khalid reached out and lightly enclosed the narrow circle of her wrist. 'Stay and talk to me for a while,' he said, and pulled her gently down on to the couch beside him.

Lorna's heart began to pound and she perched nervously on the edge of the seat. She dared not let him guess how disturbing she found his proximity. She had felt his strong attraction from their first meeting, and there was no point pretending otherwise.

Suppose he asked her out, would she go with him, even though she knew it would come to nothing? The temptation to know him better was strong, and she could not help remembering that his mother was British. Though he had affirmed he would never marry a Westerner, he might not feel the same way if he fell in love with one.

Startled at where her thoughts had taken her, she moved further away from him on the settee.

'You really are wasted here,' Khalid drawled suddenly.

'I hope your next remark isn't going to be "What's a beautiful girl like you doing in a job like this?" ' she retorted.

'That's exactly what I was going to say,' he grinned. 'But I was also going to ask if I could liven it up for you.'

'Liven it up?'

'Offer you a change of scenery for a few days —say Paris or Rome?'

One look into his deep blue eyes was sufficient for Lorna to understand the full implication of his words, as well as to understand Hassan's sly look. Her naïve daydreaming vanished. Khalid wanted her all right, but not in the way *she* wanted.

'You disappoint me,' she said in dulcet tones. 'I expected you to show a little more finesse than your brother-in-law. But my answer to you is the same one I gave to him—no.'

'A pity,' he replied matter-of-factly. 'I expected to be luckier than Hassan. After all, he's married and you were sensible to turn him down. But I have no encumbrances and I would be more than generous with you.'

'It's sweet of you to offer.' Her voice was still gentle. 'But I'm not interested. If you're desperate, though, I might be able to supply you with a couple of phone numbers of willing girls.'

He studied her thoughtfully, in no way put out by her comment.

'A man doesn't have to be desperate to want to make love to a beautiful girl like you. He would have to be out of his mind if he didn't want it.'

Lorna went to rise, intending the gesture as a termination of their conversation. But again his hand encircled her wrist, only this time his grip was not gentle but like a band of steel, and with one swift movement he pulled her to him and roughly took possession of her mouth.

She tried to pull away, but he held her so tightly to him that she could barely breathe, and his closeness made her vibrantly aware of the hard muscles of his chest and the pounding of his heart against her breasts.

She tried to turn her head away to escape his hungry mouth as it moved expertly back and forth against her own, but her frantic efforts only served to excite him further. She willed herself to relax and he took this as a sign of surrender and loosened his grip. Instantly she wrenched free of him and stood up. Her legs felt like rubber, but her eyes were blazing with a passion brought on not by desire but fury. There had been no tenderness in his touch, only naked lust, and for this she hated him.

'How dare you!' she panted.

'There was no daring required.' His pupils were dilated and his eyes still languorous as he stood up to face her. 'Don't tell me you didn't want it as much as I did? Or do you think that playing hard to get will make you more desirable to me?'

Her hand rose, and before he guessed her intention she brought it down with all her force on his tanned cheek.

Khalid stepped back, his eyes glittering with

such ferocity that she feared for her safety. His own hand lifted and she recoiled. But it was not to strike her back, as she had feared, but to rub his face where the red weals of her fingers were beginning to surface.

Lorna already regretted her action. She had behaved like a heroine in a Victorian melodrama— and a bad one at that. After all, what did a kiss— however passionate—mean these days? If she wanted to be honest with herself she knew the reason for her over-reaction. It was because Khalid would never have attempted the same intimacy with an Arab girl, and it proved how little respect he had for *her*.

'That's the first time I've been answered quite so painfully since I was a small boy,' he said ruefully. 'But a simple "no" would have served just as well.'

Anger bubbled to the surface again at his comment. He didn't even have the decency to apologise.

'I felt my answer needed reinforcing,' she retorted. 'It's time you realised that not all Western women are yours for the asking.'

'Now that *does* surprise me,' he said sarcastically, and sauntered over to the bar, where he poured himself a large brandy, first proffering the bottle towards her in a wordless question. She purposefully ignored him. Although she could have done with a drink, she had no intention of letting him know it.

'However,' he continued, 'it seems I made a mistake with you. I should have realised you weren't the type to give in to a man you barely knew.'

'Is that your idea of a compliment?' she enquired.

'If I read the expression on your face correctly, I can assume it isn't yours.'

'For once our communication is perfect,' she told him frostily. 'And for your added information, when I do "give in", as you so succinctly put it, it will be to my husband, and no one else.'

His eyes glinted and she had the impression that he found her answer amusing.

'In that case, I shan't bother you again,' he said indifferently, and turned away to set down his glass.

With as much dignity as she could muster, she walked from the room.

Although Lorna guessed that Dana's husband was partly to blame for Khalid's behaviour, she was bitterly disappointed that he had believed Hassan's lies. She realised she had made a mistake in assuming that because he was half English, he thought like a Westerner—in spite of his clearly expressed opinions to the contrary. Khalid saw women either as chattels, mistresses or—like herself—as good for a one-night stand. Why had she been stupid enough to think otherwise? Was it because she had wanted to believe it?

Her cheeks burned at the admission. Khalid's professed interest in her views over dinner had been solely for the purpose of disarming her. And she had fallen for it. But at least she had shown him that his charm didn't always work.

Momentarily she relived his kiss, and the

memory of it made her tremble. It was foolish to deny that she was physically attracted to him despite the fact that she disliked his views on everything and despised his way of life.

Until Khalid, no man had pierced her armour of sexual reserve, and she had always been in full control of her emotions. It was ironic that the one man who had succeeded in arousing her should be the one man she could never have on her own terms.

And to have him on his was something she would never do.

CHAPTER FOUR

LORNA was relieved that for the next few days she hardly saw Khalid.

When they did meet, he acted as if nothing had happened between them and treated her with the same polite friendliness as before. Neither by word or gesture did he give any indication as to whether he was still annoyed or even disappointed at her rejection of him, and she could only assume that the incident was so meaningless to him that he was able to forget it.

If only she could do the same! But unfortunately she couldn't. She was vibrantly alive to his

every look, to his every word. Had he been staying here for long, she would have been forced to
leave, and she sustained herself with the knowledge that he was soon returning to his homeland.

She also saw little of Dana. She flitted in and
out of the flat during the day, busily shopping for
presents to send home to Kuwait, and her evenings were spent dining out with Hassan and her
brother.

When they did manage to snatch some time together she noticed that the younger girl appeared
to be in exceptionally high spirits, and Lorna gave
Khalid credit for this. In spite of treating his sister
as if she were still a child, with constant teasing
and a refusal to take any of her utterances seriously, it was easy to see the deep affection he felt
for her. That was why it was difficult to understand why he had forced her into a loveless marriage.

The day before he was to leave for Kuwait,
Lorna had the afternoon off. She spent it at the
hospital, and after catching up on the gossip with
her friends, she went into Matron's office to tell
her she would soon be returning to work.

'I'm glad to hear it,' said Matron with a smile. 'I
was afraid you would be spoiled by luxury.'

'I'm not the type to be spoiled that easily,'
Lorna replied, and fleetingly wished she were.
Somehow she had the feeling that, as a lover,
Khalid would be unforgettable.

Matron was not the only person who was glad
to hear Lorna intended to leave the Rashids'.
David had constantly grumbled at her unavail-

ability and she had still not plucked up the courage to tell him she wanted to stop seeing him.

It had not been difficult to fob him off with the excuse that Dana was very demanding and gave her little opportunity to go out in the evenings. But he had been particularly insistent for the past couple of weeks, and had refused to listen to her excuses, until she had finally agreed to meet him for dinner tonight.

He was waiting for her at the entrance to Waltons, and as she greeted him she found herself contrasting his conventional good looks with Khalid's outstanding ones.

As the evening wore on she realised that even the things she had enjoyed most about their relationship now appeared mundane and boring. His humour was less sharp than Khalid's and there was nothing about him that made her aware of herself as a woman. If she felt like this after all the months they had been going out together, there was certainly no hope of anything more worthwhile developing.

It did not take David long to sense she had something on her mind.

'You haven't been listening to a word I've been saying,' he accused. 'What's the matter with you tonight?'

Lorna speared a tiny potato on her fork. 'I've been thinking how unfair it is for me to go on seeing you. I . . . I know this isn't the place to tell you, but I can't put it off any longer.'

'Have you met someone else?' he asked, instantly alert. 'Is that why you've been avoiding me?'

'There's no one else,' she said firmly. 'It's just that I know we're not right for each other.'

'Speak for yourself,' he joked, but she could see the hurt in his eyes. 'If there's no one else, why can't you go on seeing me? How can you be sure you won't grow to love me?'

'If it hasn't happened by now, it never will.' She determined not to waver in her resolve. Having plucked up the courage to tell him, she did not want him to persuade her otherwise. 'I'm sorry, David, but it's better if we don't see each other.'

'I won't give you up,' he told her doggedly. 'I'll take out other girls and you feel free to do as you please. But I still want to see you.'

It seemed easier for Lorna to give in than to continue arguing. She would have to make sure she was not available for him.

'I'll phone you in a few weeks,' he told her as he stopped his Lancia outside the block of flats in Lowndes Square. 'You're the loveliest and most intelligent girl I know, and I refuse to give up a combination like that without a fight.'

As she pressed the lift button and was whizzed up to the penthouse, she thought of his last words. At least David saw her as a person and not merely a body to be possessed without thought for what lay beneath the surface. If only Khalid had seen her in the same way! Angered at where her thoughts had taken her, she closed the front door sharply.

The apartment was in darkness except for a light glowing beneath the study door. She knocked and then opened it without waiting for a reply. Dana invariably stayed up to hear how her evenings had gone, delighted in Lorna's freedom, which was so different from her own confined upbringing.

But tonight it was not Dana who was waiting to greet her; only a grim and taut Khalid, who rose swiftly from a leather armchair near the window.

'So you're home at last! I've been waiting up to talk to you.' He glanced ostentatiously at his watch, as if it were the middle of the night instead of twelve o'clock. 'Sit down,' he commanded so fiercely that, taken by surprise, she meekly complied.

For several seconds he stared at her. Had the knowledge that she had gone out with another man aroused his jealousy to the point where he could not control it? It was an alarming yet exciting thought.

'Did you know about my sister's love affair?' he suddenly demanded.

The question was so unexpected that Lorna felt the blood drain from her cheeks. How could Dana have told him about Allan without discussing it with her first? They had spoken of the situation on so many occasions, and always reached the same conclusion; that it was best to leave things as they were until Allan left Kuwait at the end of his contract.

'I . . . I. . . .' she stammered, uncertain of what to say.

'It's obvious from your reaction that you did know,' he stormed. 'I thought you had enough sense to discourage her. But then, with your misguided views on women's rights, you probably don't see anything wrong in a wife enjoying extra-marital relationships!'

'That's a disgusting accusation!' Lorna rejoined furiously. 'The only way my views differ from yours, on that point, is that I think they apply to men as well as women. The last thing I'd do would be to encourage your sister to have an affair. And for your information, in spite of the fact that I know how unhappy she is, I've done my best to stop her from doing anything foolish. If anyone's to blame, it's you. If she'd been allowed to choose a husband for herself, this would never have happened.'

'That's exactly what I expected you to say; but freedom of choice hasn't made *your* countrywomen any the happier.'

'At least we have the *freedom* to get divorced,' she pointed out scathingly. 'We aren't forced to live with a man we loathe.' Angrily she tossed back a lock of hair that had fallen over her face. 'In your country marriage vows only mean to honour and obey—it's about time you let love in as well.'

He gave a weary sigh. 'It's useless to argue with you. We will never agree. But now I must decide what is the best thing to do for Dana.'

'How much did she tell you?' Lorna asked hesitantly, still hoping the girl had had the sense not to give him Allan's name.

'Everything.'

'I see.' Lorna's lips went dry and she licked them before speaking. 'Then ... then you——'

'I know they met when they shared a table over lunch at Harrods,' Khalid went on as if she had not spoken. 'And that she has been using her friends as an alibi to see him during the day.'

Lorna could not believe what she was hearing. Why on earth had Dana woven this fantastic web of lies to her brother? She was soon enlightened.

'The only thing for me to do is to take her back home with me. I have promised not to tell Hassan about this—this relationship, and she has promised not to see the man again nor to communicate with him.'

'You mean you're taking her back to Kuwait?' Lorna asked, the penny dropping immediately.

'Yes,' he said abruptly. 'But not without a tremendous row.' A tight smile appeared at the corner of his lips, though it did not lighten his features. 'She fought against going, of course. I never realised my sister could throw such a tantrum.'

Her performance must have been worthy of Sarah Bernhardt, Lorna thought grimly, and marvelled at Dana's duplicity. How angry Khalid would be if he knew that in taking his sister back to her own country he was doing exactly as she wished! Had it not been that her own brother was involved in Dana's scheme—even though she was certain he knew nothing about it—Lorna would have enjoyed the knowledge that Khalid had been duped. As it was, her fear for Allan was predominant.

'I had to promise Dana I would persuade you to return with us to Kuwait,' Khalid broke into her thoughts. 'For some reason she didn't want to ask you herself.'

I'll bet she didn't, Lorna thought, but kept her face expressionless.

'I hope you'll try to forget *our* differences and think only of my sister's happiness,' he went on. 'If you do come back with us it need only be for a short time—until she's got over this affair. She's convinced she cannot manage without you.'

The idea of living in Kuwait and seeing Khalid, if only occasionally, made her so fearful that she instinctively shook her head.

'It's out of the question,' she replied. 'I'm fond of Dana, as you know, but I've planned to return to the hospital.'

The tanned face in front of her darkened, and the lines on it grew harsh. Seeing them she knew what an implacable enemy he would make; an enemy who could destroy Allan. And there was no doubt that Allan was the reason Dana had perpetrated this whole charade. Lorna thought of the harsh Koranic laws regarding adulterous relationships, and knew how dangerous her brother's position was. Although his love for Dana was still unconsummated, if they were caught alone together, who would believe them? At least if she went back with Dana and stayed in Kuwait until her brother's contract ran out in a few months, she

could ensure that neither of them took unneces-
sary risks.

Why couldn't Dana have waited until Allan
returned to this country? Had their separation
caused her more heartache than Lorna had suspected? And didn't this make it even more imperative that she herself remain close at hand to
ensure that Dana was continually aware of the
dangerous path she was treading?

'Well?' Khalid asked. 'Will you accompany
her? I'll double your salary if you do agree.'

'That won't be necessary,' Lorna said sharply.
'My concern for Dana's happiness is the only reason I need for changing my mind.'

'Thank you. I realise what an effort it will be
for you to live in a country whose male citizens
you regard as archaic.'

She refused to rise to the bait, and standing up,
turned towards the door. But as he had done once
before, he stopped her by reaching out and clasp-
ing her wrists.

'I know you planned to go back to the hospital,
and that it might mean losing your position there.
Because of that, I insist you let me compensate
you financially if you are unable to find a similar
position when you return.'

Lorna gently extricated herself from his grip. 'I
appreciate the offer, but there's no need for it.
There's no shortage of jobs—only nurses to fill
them.'

'You won't be expected to look after the baby
when we go home,' he said abruptly. 'We have
servants of our own to take care of her. All I want

is for you to keep Dana's mind occupied and to let me know if you think she's not adjusting to the situation.'

'What would you do then?' Lorna asked casually.

'I'm not sure.'

'I don't like the idea of spying on your sister.'

'You wouldn't be. But Dana is still a child in many ways and she needs protecting.' As if the word 'protecting' sparked off a memory in him, his eyes dropped to Lorna's mouth. 'You need have no fear for *your* safety when you are in my country. I will treat you with as much respect as if you were one of our own women.'

Spots of red flagged her cheeks and she avoided his gaze. 'Thank you.'

She went towards the door, but his next words stopped her.

'It is generous of you to accept my word. I hope this means you will now allow us to become friends?'

He sounded so sincere that Lorna found herself forgiving him. It was not in her nature to bear a grudge, and if she was going to live in his home for some months to come, it would be better if there was no antagonism between them.

'I'm perfectly willing to try,' she said. 'I partly blame your brother-in-law for the other evening. If he hadn't encouraged you to believe——'

'I didn't need any encouragement from Hassan to want to kiss you,' Khalid interrupted, his eyes sparkling. 'I wanted to do so from the moment I saw you without your disguise. But as I've just said, you need have no fear for the future. I shall respect your wishes not to make love to you again.' He eyed her pensively for a moment, and his self-confidence appeared to slip. 'I suppose you think I'm wrong to try to save Dana's marriage?'

'Does it matter what *I* think?' Lorna asked, afraid that an honest answer might break their fragile truce.

'If it didn't, I wouldn't have asked you,' he answered irritably.

Lorna took a deep breath and geared herself up for a few nasty minutes. If he was sincerely interested in her opinion, perhaps she stood a chance —a slender one, of course, but a chance nonetheless—of being able to change his outlook, or at least give him food for thought.

'I don't think Dana has much of a marriage to save,' she said aloud. 'If it weren't for her having to leave Amina, if she left Hassan, nothing would induce her to remain with him.' She paused to allow her words to sink in. 'She's dreadfully unhappy, Khalid. If you could persuade Hassan to let her keep the baby——'

'That is impossible,' he interrupted forcefully. 'It is contrary to our tradition.'

'Traditions are constantly being broken by progress.'

'Not always to the benefit of people. A father has first call on his children.'

'And a mother?'

'She should know where her duty lies.'

'Regardless of love?'

'A woman's first love is to her children. To her

husband she owes her duty and her obedience.'

'Oh, you're impossible!' Lorna stormed.

'Because I value tradition? Because I believe that women are weak creatures who need a strong hand to guide them? You might be able to use your beauty to persuade me of many things, but on one thing I will remain firm: a father has the sole right to his children.'

Hearing this, Lorna recognised the futility of arguing further. Khalid might believe he was adhering to tradition when he spoke in this way, but she knew he was impelled by the hurt that had been inflicted on him by his own mother, who had so heartlessly abandoned him.

'Perhaps I shouldn't have persuaded you to come back with us.' Khalid was speaking again. 'Your views are so different from ours that you're hardly the right influence on my sister.'

'Given time, I might still be the right influence on you,' she said tartly. 'You are half English, even though you prefer to forget it.'

His indrawn breath was audible. 'Don't make the mistake of judging me by the colour of my eyes. I am my father's son in every sense of the word.'

'You are your mother's son too.'

Khalid's eyes flashed dangerously and she saw they had gone paler. They changed colour with his mood, glinting ice blue when he was angry, a deeper blue when he was teasing, and almost cobalt when he was aroused. Hurriedly she pushed the last thought from her mind. At this moment he was in a furious temper, and she regretted her outspokenness. Probably no woman had ever spoken to him so frankly, and she could not help admiring the effort he was making to keep his temper. She only hoped she had not gone too far and that they were not in for another row.

But she had no need to worry.

'It appears we've reached an impasse,' he replied tonelessly, 'so we will not continue with this subject. But if nothing else has been achieved, at least we've proved we can argue without coming to blows.'

Accepting the fact that her opinions had fallen on deaf ears, she nodded. Khalid had controlled his temper only because he wanted to establish a workable relationship between them. He knew that after the other evening, this was the only approach that would succeed if he wanted her to stay in Kuwait with his sister. But he would never be swayed by the view of a woman, however just. He lived in a man's world, in which females were very much second-class citizens. A passport to happiness in Kuwait meant obedience and acquiescence, and the sooner she accepted this, the happier she would be there.

Murmuring goodnight, she left the room. His presence seemed to permeate her own room and she chided herself for still being so susceptible to him. It was wrong for one man to be endowed with so much: looks, money and intelligence. He had taken hold of her senses and unless she could stop herself thinking of him—in any context other than a casual one—she was in for a great deal of heartache.

Even in bed she could not relax. The moment she did, Khalid threatened to take possession of her, causing her to experience such a longing for him that she was horrified with herself. She barely knew him. Yet this did not stop her from thinking like an erotic teenager. Wryly she knew she was lucky he had not made any advances towards her this evening. Had he done, she might not have found it so easy to resist him a second time. Because of this she wondered if it was not foolish to return to Kuwait with him, no matter how worried she was about her brother. Yet if she didn't go and anything happened to jeopardise Allan's career, she would never forgive herself. She sighed heavily, and reached up to turn off the bedside light. With a bit of luck she might only have to stay a short time. Perhaps when Dana and Allan saw each other again they would find that their love was not as strong as they imagined. Although she knew the old adage, that absence made the heart grow fonder, she prayed with all her heart that in this instance it had not.

If only she did not have to go to Kuwait! If only Allan were already back in England. If only. . . .

CHAPTER FIVE

THE next few days were hectic. Lorna drove down to Bournemouth to say goodbye to her parents who, after their initial surprise at her sudden change of plans, delighted in the fact that she would soon be seeing Allan.

She maintained the pretence of Dana's encounter with another man here as the reason for the return to Kuwait, though Mrs Masters felt it would have been more sensible for the girl to have gone on a holiday with her husband first.

'She misses her family and friends more than anything,' Lorna lied. 'That's why she's going back there.'

'What is Mr Rashid like?' asked her mother.

'Quite nice, in a fleshy-lipped way.'

Mrs Masters raised her blonde eyebrows. She was very much like Lorna in looks, although her hair was tinged with silver and her figure had filled out with middle-age.

'As long as you don't get bowled over by all that money and luxury living. England is your home, Lorna, and you wouldn't be happy living anywhere else—even if it were a palace.'

'Don't be so sure about that.' Lorna laughed

when she saw her mother's expression. 'Don't worry, Mummy—I'm too old to be swept off my feet by a sheikh.'

'I hope that also applies to Mrs Rashid's brother. When you were here last you gave me the impression that you found him very attractive.'

'He is. But he's made it quite clear that Western women are good for one thing only, and a wedding ring is not included in the proposal.'

A quick trip to Knightsbridge was next on Lorna's agenda, to add to a rather depleted wardrobe. Her parents had insisted on giving her a large cheque to treat herself to some good clothes, and with unaccustomed extravagance she shopped until she had spent the lot.

Hassan had not appeared the least surprised when Khalid had told him he was taking Dana home with him for a holiday. He was so used to taking orders from his brother-in-law that he accepted his pronouncement without question, and was probably quite pleased to be left to his own devices. Now he could spend every night away from home if he wished.

Dana was delighted that Lorna had agreed to accompany them back to Kuwait, and good-naturedly accepted Lorna's lecture on the dangers of the situation ahead.

'But I had to find an excuse for going back,' she said sweetly, 'and since Khalid knows I can't bear Hassan, it seemed logical to pretend I was in love with someone else. As I am,' she emphasised for good measure.

'As you have no right to be,' Lorna added.

'I won't do anything to harm Allan,' Dana said instantly. 'But I couldn't bear to be so far away from him. When you're in love you will know what I mean. Thinking of him turns my bones to water. Remembering his voice makes my heart race like an engine.'

'Nonsense,' said Lorna in her briskest voice, refusing to acknowledge that a certain black-haired, golden-skinned man had exactly the same effect on herself. 'What would you have done if I hadn't decided to go back to Kuwait with you?' she asked.

'But you are coming,' Dana replied. 'With you in our house, Allan can visit me at any time. After all, we know what a loving brother he is.'

'Don't you feel any guilt towards Hassan?' Lorna reprimanded.

'The only guilt I feel is towards Allan. I know that when he sees me he will want me, and because he's too moral to give in, he will suffer.'

'He'll suffer all right,' Lorna said grimly. 'But if you know that, why go back?'

'Because I cannot help myself.'

At the end of the week the Rashids' chauffeur-driven Mercedes took them to the airport, with another limousine following with the remaining cases.

At Heathrow they stopped at the special Concorde entrance, where an official in civilian clothes summoned porters and then led them in. After the usual formalities were completed they were ushered into the Concorde lounge, where waiters proffered cocktails and canapés.

'You can call anywhere in the world free, by courtesy of British Airways,' Khalid informed them as he saw them seated in one of the many comfortable armchairs—and then promptly left to telephone New York.

Lorna could not suppress a smile. Even multi-millionaires enjoyed something for nothing!

With a glass of champagne in one hand and her mouth full of caviar, she did not care if Concorde never left the ground. The lounge was so restful and soundless, save for the purr of telephone dials, that she enjoyed wallowing in the sheer luxury of it. But their flight was called on time. What else could one have expected from the pride of British Airways?

The plane was nearly full, and the passengers were mostly Arab men in national dress. The seating was narrower than in a conventional plane and disappointingly functional. The hostesses, who wore the formal standard blue uniform of the airline, gave each passenger a pair of flamboyant royal blue slippers with the silver British Concorde crest, explaining that they were needed because the height tightened one's shoes. Later they also distributed little plastic-crested briefcases as an additional souvenir.

Dana and Lorna sat together, with the baby on Lorna's lap despite Dana's protest.

'She's in my charge until we reach Kuwait and your own staff take over,' Lorna insisted.

But in fact she did not have to hold Amina for long, for soon after take-off, one of the steward-

esses asked them if they would care to place her
carrycot on the seat behind, which was unoccu-
pied. Lorna willingly accepted the offer. Khalid
was seated across the aisle from them, but had
immersed himself in documents and did not lift
his head until lunch was served, though even then
he only conversed with his sister.

When they reached Bahrein they were afforded
the same royal treatment as at Heathrow. Unfortunately it was now dark, because Bahrein was
three hours ahead of English time, and Lorna saw
little except the scrubland bordering the airport.

'It feels like autumn,' she murmured to Khalid
as they both descended Concorde's steps to the
accompaniment of a chill breeze.

'The evenings are always cold in the desert,' he
explained. 'But during the day you will find it hot
enough to need air-conditioning.'

Their connecting flight to Kuwait was already
waiting for them. The al Hashibs' private Lear jet
stood on the tarmac, fuelled and ready to go as
soon as their luggage was collected, and within
half an hour they were on their way in the
luxuriously fitted plane.

It did not fly at the speed of Concorde, but it
was less noisy and far more comfortable. The re-
clining seats were like armchairs and covered in
an orange tweed, the colour exactly matching the
al Hashib emblem of a hawk.

Dana dozed and Khalid again returned to his
papers. The baby was fractious and Lorna spent
most of her time trying to keep her amused. Since
the evening Khalid had asked her to return to Ku-

wait with them, she had not seen him alone. He had gone to Paris until the day before their departure from London, and even on his last night he had dined out. Lorna sourly admitted that he was not so much deliberately avoiding her, as that having accomplished his aim, he saw no reason to go out of his way to be more than polite.

It was nearly midnight when they landed at Kuwait. The airport was small, ultra-modern and spotlessly clean. Several dark-skinned men rushed forward as soon as they entered the building, and gabbled in Arabic to Khalid who, she gathered, was giving instructions to his servants about their luggage.

To Lorna's surprise, Allan was not there to greet her. She had telephoned to let him know she was coming over with Dana, and although he had sounded delighted, his conversation had been stilted. But he had promised to meet her, though their hour of arrival was late. The mystery was soon solved when Khalid was handed a message by a receptionist, which he quickly read.

'Your brother sends his apologies,' he told her. 'He had to do an emergency Caesarian operation and he's been detained at the hospital. He'll be over to see you in the morning.'

Dana's face showed her disappointment, but she turned away to speak to one of the servants so that Khalid did not notice anything amiss. Swiftly he propelled them towards the exit and into a large white Cadillac, while their luggage was piled into a Rolls Corniche parked behind. Trust Khalid to use a Rolls as a van!

The journey to the suburb of Salamiyya took only half an hour through the well-lit boulevards of Kuwait. Lorna glimpsed tall, modern buildings and lots of open spaces with grass and trees surrounding them, but they were mere etchings in the dark.

'Where's the old part of the city?' she asked.

'Unfortunately there's very little of it left,' Khalid said. 'Nowadays a building that has stood for twenty years is considered antique. We have tried to eradicate our past too quickly for my liking, and with some disastrous results.' He waved an arm. 'Look at these glass and concrete monstrosities.'

'What did you have before?'

He took the point and his teeth gleamed in the semi-darkness of the car. 'We didn't all live in tents, you know. Many Arab families here have had great wealth for many years.'

Lorna bit back the comment that now some of them had more money than sense. Some things were better left unsaid.

'You'll also see lots of unfinished houses and apartments all over the city,' Dana joined in the conversation. 'It's a national mania to want something bigger and better all the time.'

They were now speeding along the dual carriageway that bordered the seafront. It was a busy main road and traffic roared past in an incessant stream despite the late hour.

They finally drew up alongside a white fortress-like wall in which were set wrought-iron gates

that glided open electronically. The car drove between them and into a circular driveway, giving
Lorna her first breathtaking glimpse of the sprawl-
ing villa. It was single-storeyed and Moorish in
style, the smooth façade gleaming like a pearl in
the moonlight. An arched verandah ran its entire
length and long narrow windows were decorated
with elegant wrought-iron grilles.

But she was left little time to linger and admire,
and was shepherded swiftly into the rectangular
hall.

A solemn-faced butler in white jacket and
striped trousers stood by the open carved teak
door, giving orders to the servants who were
carrying in the carloads of luggage. An elderly
woman in traditional Arab garb stood beside
him, but as soon as Dana came up the marble
steps she fell on her, kissing her and making a
great fuss and noise over the baby.

'My old nurse,' Dana explained to Lorna when
she finally managed to pull herself away. 'She'll
be taking care of Amina.'

Lorna thought she looked too ancient for the
demanding task of caring for an active nine-
month-old child, and Dana read the uncertainty
on her face.

'Don't worry,' she added reassuringly. 'She's
not as old as she looks, and her daughter Farida
will be helping out as well.'

'Don't stand there talking,' Khalid interrupted
his sister. 'Mother is in bed, but she won't sleep
until we've seen her.' He looked at Lorna. 'I'm

sure you must be tired, so Mustafa will show you to your room. He speaks fairly good English and if you need anything, ask him.'

Lorna turned to move away, but Khalid's voice stopped her.

'Please don't unpack your clothes. One of the servants will do it for you in the morning.'

'I'm quite able to manage on my own.'

'I'm sure you are. But the servants will see it as a sign that you don't trust them.' His smile was dry. 'Life here is different from England. A young woman of your class is not expected to do anything for herself, and as you are here as a friend of the family, I must ask you to follow our customs.'

He strode away and Lorna, left alone with the butler, glanced slowly around. The entrance hall contained no furniture, but the cream stone walls were hung with large modern paintings and free-standing sculptures dotted the blue terracotta tiled floor. Although her knowledge of art was limited, she recognised the work of Reg Butler, Kandinsky and Mondriaan, and was suitably impressed.

The wall of glass opposite her parted under electric power as she followed the manservant into an outside courtyard planted with exotic trees and shrubs. Two flat, octagonal marble fountains of space-age design were inset into the white gravel, and floodlit, so that the water glittered below. The arched and pillared terrace was lit by a multitude of lanterns, although the rooms beyond them were in darkness. More glass glided open and she entered a wide corridor with a seemingly endless array of white louvred doors.

'All bedrooms here,' the butler explained, and opened one, standing back for her to enter.

The first thing she saw was her luggage, neatly stacked and waiting for her; the next thing she noticed was the pale sycamore furniture and thick, almond green lush carpet and drapes.

'Is anything I get you?' the man asked with a smile, showing a set of pearly white teeth too perfect to be his own.

'No, thank you.' Lorna smiled.

'You want later, you ring bell by bed.' With a salaam he glided out.

Lorna unpacked her smallest valise, which contained her nightclothes. In spite of Khalid's warning, she was damned if she would sleep in the nude just to please the servants. They would have to be content with her remaining three cases in the morning.

In spite of being exhausted she had a bath, and found it difficult not to linger in the lightly scented water of the pink marble sunken tub. But after a quick dip she thankfully slipped into bed and luxuriated in the feel of pure silk sheets upon her limbs. If Ann or David could see her now!

Her eyes were heavy, yet sleep did not come, for her mind was too full of the day's events and the strangeness of her surroundings. She was glad Allan had not been at the airport to meet them, for Khalid might have noticed something amiss. His eyes were sharp and Dana was not good at hiding her feelings.

Unlike herself, of course. Fortunately he had no idea she found him attractive. She turned restlessly. He was not a man who would take no for an answer—he probably rarely needed to—and if he ever guessed how susceptible she was to him, he would exploit the situation to his advantage.

It was a dismaying prospect, for she was by no means convinced she could resist him if he turned on his charm again. Yet resist him she must. His interest in her was purely sexual and could lead only to bed—never the altar.

This was something she must never forget. It was the only way in which she could manage to keep the full flame of her resistance burning.

CHAPTER SIX

LORNA was roused the following morning by a knock at her door, and glancing at the small bedside clock, she saw it was past nine.

'Come on, lazybones,' Dana cried gaily, darting in. 'It's a beautiful day and I don't want you to waste a moment of it.'

'I thought the weather was always good here,' said Lorna.

'Not in winter. We have the odd rainstorm or it's too windy to sit outside.' Dana went over to the windows and pulled open the curtains letting in a sudden blaze of sunshine. 'Do hurry and get dressed.'

'It's not the sun you're afraid of missing,' Lorna replied, forcing herself out of bed. 'It's Allan. But for God's sake be careful when you see him. Even if Khalid isn't around, remember the servants have eyes and ears too.'

'Don't worry,' Dana reassured her. 'I've no intention of ruining my wonderful plan by doing anything foolish. Khalid's already left for the office, so we shouldn't be disturbed.'

She waited while Lorna dressed, chatting excitedly all the time. Rarely had she looked so carefree, and once again Lorna found it easy to understand why Allan had fallen in love with her. She was a warm, uncomplicated girl, with a sense of fun that would complement his more serious nature.

Lorna's first glimpse of the immense living area that ran the entire breadth of the house and overlooked the ocean was as breathtaking as her first view of the house itself. It must have been some fifty feet square and was approached by a small entrance hall, which in turn led on to a wide gallery. On less-than-sunny days this section could be reduced in size by sliding glass walls, and it was indeed multi-purpose, for part of the gallery was an outdoor dining-room overlooking the garden.

In the living room itself, chunky white wicker chairs and pale tweed-covered settees were grouped informally to provide four or five conversation areas, and the predominating colours of turquoise, orange and white harmonised perfectly with the blue terracotta tiling of the floor—which also ran throughout the entire house.

'Khalid has fabulous taste,' Dana stated matter-of-factly, noting Lorna's wide-eyed admiration of the fine Art Nouveau decor and the equally fine ornaments that embellished it: lalique vases, a chess set in gold and enamel inset with turquoise jewels and a variety of mirrors all made by the top craftsmen of that era.

'He approved every item of furniture himself, and several of the ideas were his,' Dana added.

'He must have inherited his talent from his mother,' Lorna commented.

'Don't say that in front of him,' Dana warned, and led the way out of the living-room to a flower-filled patio set with more wicker furniture.

Here, a table was set for breakfast, and Lorna was surprised to find the cooking decidedly English.

'This was laid on for you,' Dana informed her, sipping coffee and watching Lorna tackle scrambled eggs. 'Khalid thought you would prefer not to try our food on your first morning.'

Lorna was gratified by Khalid's thoughtfulness. 'I assumed he'd consider running a home to be women's work.'

'He does. But he hasn't found a woman he can trust to run it as efficiently as he does. He's terribly particular, and has all the servants trained like old English retainers.'

'Doesn't your mother mind his interference?'

'My mother has her own separate quarters, and she does as she pleases there.'

Lorna looked perplexed.

'Khalid entertains men and women together here and my mother would never join a social gathering of mixed company,' Dana explained. 'That's why she keeps to her own quarters unless Khalid specifically invites her to come out.'

'Does that mean she only sees women?'

'Yes, and so do most of her friends.'

'Doesn't she *ever* go out?'

'You can't keep her in,' the other girl laughed. 'One of her few concessions to the modern world is to be driven round the city. Instead of whiling away her hours at home, as she used to, she visits her friends and sees the new world that's grown up outside. She also adores gossiping for hours on the telephone. In my father's day she would never have been allowed to do either.'

'Considering your father broke with tradition by taking an Englishwoman as his first wife, I'm surprised he was so strict with his second,' said Lorna.

Dana looked amused. 'You must realise that the men here have always had double standards. Away from home they live as they please, but in Kuwait they toe the line and demand the same of their women.'

'I'm not a Women's Libber,' Lorna rejoined, 'but you could do with starting a movement here. It strikes me there's only one thing to be in Kuwait—and that's a man.'

After they had finished eating, Dana suggested taking Lorna to meet her mother.

'I've left instructions that we're to be told as soon as Allan arrives,' she said.

Madam al Hashib was having coffee when they entered her living room. She was in her late forties, plump, with an unlined face, and had the same saucer-like brown eyes as her daughter and granddaughter. Surprisingly she was in European clothes: a silk shirtwaister and high-heeled shoes, and she wore her short, dark hair in the latest style.

'*Ahlan wa sahlan,*' she said with a friendly smile, and shook Lorna's hand before giving her daughter an affectionate kiss on the cheek.

'That means a smiling welcome,' Dana translated. 'Unfortunately my mother speaks very little English.'

Madam al Hashib continued talking to her daughter in gentle tones, but with an air of lively interest, her hands fluttering in small precise gestures to emphasise her words.

'She's delighted to hear your brother works at the Saud hospital,' Dana told Lorna with pretended innocence. 'She wants you to feel free to invite him here.'

Lorna could have wrung Dana's neck, but instead acknowledged the woman's offer with a smile of thanks.

For the next few minutes mother and daughter spoke in Arabic and Lorna studied the room. Expensively furnished, but old-fashioned, it would

not have been out of place in Victorian England,
crowded as it was with bric-à-brac and photo-
graphs. The contrast to the rest of the house was
so great that it was obvious Khalid had had no
hand in the decor here.

A knock at the door made her turn round, and
a servant entered and announced that Allan had
arrived.

Dana tried to keep her expression noncommit-
tal, but she could not hide the sparkle in her eyes,
and with a murmured excuse to her mother she
followed Lorna out.

Allan was waiting for them in the living-room
and for a brief instance he stared silently at Dana
before stepping forward to hug his sister. Close to
him, Lorna sensed his tension and her fears for
him grew.

'It's wonderful to see you,' he murmured.
'You're looking great.'

'So are you,' she said, although he didn't.

He was too thin and too pale, with fine lines
around his eyes that should not have been there.
Darling Allan, she thought, and could cheerfully
have consigned Dana to the nether regions. But
turning to look at the girl, her sympathy was
alerted, for Dana was staring at Allan with a
world of love in her eyes.

'Aren't you going to say hullo to me?' Dana
asked.

'Of course.' His voice was husky, stilted.
'You're looking very well. Are you planning to
stay long?'

'Until *you* return to England.'

His face contorted. 'Dana, don't. You mustn't say that.'

'Why not? Have you stopped loving me?'

He flung an anguished look at his sister, and Lorna stared back at him wordlessly. But her expression made it clear that Dana had put her in the picture.

'Couldn't you have persuaded her not to come back?' he demanded, his voice still husky.

'No, I couldn't.' Lorna glanced at her watch. 'I'm taking a stroll around the garden. But I won't be away for more than ten minutes—it's too dangerous for you to be alone for longer than that.'

She hurried out, knowing that the moment she disappeared from sight they would be in each other's arms. It came home to her that she was a party to Dana's deceit, and her conscience, which had pricked her in England, now began to jab more sharply. Yet short of telling Khalid the truth there was nothing she could do except watch and make sure that neither Allan nor Dana did anything that would arouse the wrath of this harshly rigid society.

By the time she returned to the living-room Allan and Dana were sitting circumspectly on two different settees, but the girl's brown eyes were glowing, and even Allan could not hide his joy.

'With you in the house,' he said to his sister, 'I'll at least be able to come here without arousing suspicion.'

'That depends how often you come.'

'Every day,' Dana said before he could reply.

'No.' Allan ran his fingers through his hair. It was several shades darker than Lorna's, and his eyes did not have the same violet tinge. But it was obvious they were brother and sister, for they had the same supple grace of movement, though Allan was just under six feet.

'We've got to be sensible about things, Dana,' he went on. 'You're married and——'

'I'll run away from Hassan and take Amina with me. I'll hide and they'll never find me.'

'I'm afraid I *can't* hide,' Allan reminded her. 'Besides, it wouldn't work. You'd never be happy living that kind of life.'

'What life do I have now?' she cried, her large eyes shining with tears. She tried to blink them away, but the flow increased and she gave a little sob and ran from the room.

'How in heaven's name did you get involved in this mess?' Lorna asked tartly, trying not to feel sympathetic as she saw the strained expression on her brother's face. 'I thought you were far too sensible.'

'So did I,' he sighed. 'It all started so casually that I was in love before I realised it.'

'Hassan will never let her go,' Lorna stated. 'She's his meal ticket. It's only Khalid who can set her free.'

'He'll never do that. He has fixed ideas of a woman's place and nothing will change him. If he genuinely cared for Dana's happiness he could arrange a divorce for her and make sure she kept Amina.'

'Hassan's also a cousin,' Lorna pointed out. 'So family honour is involved too.'

'Khalid's rigid with his damned honour,' Allan muttered fiercely. 'It's made him unable to think in humanistic terms.'

'I know. I've clashed with him more than once.'

'I shouldn't think that went down well with his holiness. He's used to women keeping their opinions to themselves.' There was a pause. 'Let's forget this mess, shall we? Tell me all the news from home. I know the parents are well, because I spoke to them last week, but I haven't heard from David for some time. How are things between you two?'

Lorna felt a pang of guilt at the mention of David's name. She had only told him she was going to Kuwait the evening before her departure, calling him on the telephone to do so. He had wanted to come over to say goodbye, but she had pleaded packing to do, and though he had known it was an excuse, he had accepted it.

'David and I are just good friends,' she murmured.

'Pity,' Allan commented. 'It would have been great to have married you off to my best friend. Anyone else on the horizon?'

Lorna shook her head, though for some reason the mocking face of Khalid loomed vividly before her.

'I'm fancy free,' she said with determination. 'If you know any eligible bachelors, you can fix me up with some dates.'

'The problem will be to keep them away from

you! Unattached European women are at a premium here.'

'What about the nurses in the hospital?'

'There aren't enough to go around.' He glanced at the door, then rose. 'I can't wait for Dana. I have an operation scheduled.'

Lorna walked with him across the vast room and watched from the hall as he eased himself into a red Toyota coupé parked in the driveway beneath a palm tree. The car had just disappeared when Dana's high heels could be heard tapping on the floor, and Lorna swung round, relieved to see the girl was in control of herself and smiling.

'I feel so happy now,' she said softly, linking her arm affectionately with Lorna's as they went inside. 'Seeing Allan has made me so contented.'

Lorna doubted if this contentment would last. Their love was too strong for passions to remain unsatisfied, and she dreaded to think what the final outcome might be.

'Shall we have a swim and then lunch by the pool?' Dana asked. 'I don't know about you, but I feel too tired to do anything except laze.'

'Suits me. But why don't we swim in the sea? It's far more invigorating.'

Dana was horrified at the suggestion.

'No Kuwaiti girl would wear a swimming costume in public. If she were seen by a man other than her husband, she would bring shame on herself and her family. We do as we please when we're abroad, but when we live here, we have to conform.'

'Do you mind if I go?'

'I don't think you should. The men here aren't used to seeing women in swimsuits.'

'But there isn't a soul on the beach.'

'We still can't control trespassers.'

'You're not suggesting I'll be molested?'

Dana nodded. 'There have been a few cases of rape when Western women haven't respected our conventions. Don't forget it's only the rich Kuwaitis who travel abroad and have girl-friends. Those who don't, live like monks until they marry. That's why they marry so young. We also have religious fanatics who will stop at nothing if they see anyone flouting their laws.'

Dana was painting such a lurid picture that Lorna did not believe it. Nevertheless she respected her friend's wishes and sat by the pool with her.

They lazed away the rest of the morning until servants brought them a meal of fresh prawn salad and a dessert of exotic imported fruits. Afterwards Lorna dozed off in the warm sunshine. In spite of her fair skin she tanned easily, but all the same she heeded Dana's warning and kept her head covered with a large straw hat. The sun had a burning intensity here that she had not encountered before.

When she awoke she was surprised to find herself alone. Glancing at the time she saw it was nearly five. She must have been more tired than she thought, for she had slept for over two hours.

Dana reappeared a few minutes later, fully dressed. 'I have to take Amina over to my in-laws,' she explained. 'You're very welcome to join us if you wish.'

'If you don't mind I'd like to sort out my clothes. They've been unpacked and pressed, but I want to rearrange them.'

'You won't miss anything by not coming,' Dana muttered. 'My father-in-law doesn't know how to make light conversation, and my mother-in-law has the personality of a mouse.'

After she had gone, Lorna settled back again in her chair. It was quite perfect by the pool. It was tiled completely in mosaic and kidney-shaped. There was a diving-board at the far end as well as changing-rooms with showers. The water emitted the same delightful fragrance she had noticed in the bath the previous night, and together with the clusters of pink and white waterlilies floating on a raised dais in the centre, added an exotic touch. Khalid had omitted nothing in his search for perfection, except perhaps a swan for his mini-lake.

As the sun sank lower, shadows flitted across the water, and putting on a towelling jacket that matched her scarlet bikini, Lorna made her way across the grass and past a clump of trees to the beach. It was completely deserted, as was the sea, except for a dhow sailing low on the horizon. The coastline was flat as far as the eye could see, and although a busy highway ran along it leading into the city, this end was almost devoid of traffic.

Dana had told her that this area, near the point of Ras al Ardh, was not only the smartest but also the most desirable residential district, since houses here could catch the cool breezes off the sea. Khalid's was the last one to be built along this stretch of coast and though work had started on another mansion some way up, for the moment his position was idyllically peaceful.

She moved across the sand. It was soft underfoot and dazzlingly pale. Close to, the ocean was crystal clear and she slipped off her sandals and let it lap gently over her feet. It was not as warm as she had assumed, but it was marvellously refreshing. Ignoring Dana's earlier warning, she dropped her jacket on the sand and ran quickly into the water.

Lorna swam quite a distance, and then floated on her back, allowing the current to bring her in. It was only as she did so that she noticed a man in a white dashdasha, headdress flying behind him, striding purposefully towards her. He must have been driving by and spotted her as she went into the water.

In spite of the warmth of the last rays of the sun, Lorna felt herself growing cold. Other than the two of them the beach was still completely deserted, and they could not be seen from the house. Besides, who was there to miss her?

Swiftly she ran out of the sea and across the sand to where she had left her jacket. The man started to move towards her and she turned and headed in the direction of the house. But the silver sand that had previously felt as light as silk against her feet now seemed to hold her in its grip like cement, making each step an effort of will. However quickly she moved, her pursuer appeared to be gaining on her, and when she stumbled and fell, her heart began to pound with uncontrollable fear.

Momentarily she closed her eyes and tried to regain her breath, but before she could raise herself again and run, strong hands gripped her shoulders. She gave a sharp scream of fear and her assailant tugged her to her feet angrily.

The action released her from the paralysis of fright and she struggled wildly in his hold, shouting and pummelling on his chest as hard as she could, at the same time aiming sharp blows on his shins with her feet.

'For God's sake open your eyes,' a harsh male voice ordered. 'It's me—Khalid!'

For an instant the words did not penetrate, but the fact that they were English ones reassured her enough for her fear to lessen. As it did, the meaning of them came home to her, and she collapsed against his chest as limply as a rag doll.

Khalid held her close, and beneath the fine cotton of his robe she felt his heart beating as rapidly as her own.

'I . . . I didn't realise it was you,' she said breathlessly. 'I . . . thought . . . in your dashdasha. . . .'

'You're lucky it *was* me,' he replied, still holding her. 'Didn't Dana tell you not to come on the beach alone?'

'Yes, but——'

'Yes, but——' he repeated angrily. 'Don't you ever do as you're told?'

She ignored this. 'How did you know where to find me?'

'One of the servants told me you hadn't gone out with Dana, and when I couldn't find you in the house or gardens I suspected you had come out here.'

He gazed down at her and his eyes, which had so recently held anger, were glinting with another emotion. 'I don't normally find that the sight of me induces women to panic and run—quite the opposite, in fact.'

'Naturally.'

'Except for *you*,' he added. 'But at least this time I didn't get my face slapped.'

'Not so far.'

Her words served to remind him he was still holding her near-naked body in his arms, and he stepped back instantly.

'I think we both need a drink,' he said stiffly, and turned away from her.

In silence they returned to the house, each occupied with their own thoughts. Lorna could not suppress a self-satisfied smile at her own. She had finally managed to make this self-possessed man lose his cool, though he was still not certain why he had. Surely a near-naked female did not hold any mystery for him? Or had he been worried in case she had been scared he would take advantage of the situation?

She was surprised that no such thought had occurred to her. She knew he still wanted her, but she also knew he would never take an unwilling woman. He was too proud, as well as too used to subservience. Because of this, her earlier rejection of him made it all the more necessary for him to be absolutely sure of her before he made another approach.

Seated in the living-room, after changing into a floral skirt and matching tee-shirt, she watched as he expertly mixed her a fruit drink laced with champagne.

In Western clothes he had looked handsome, but in his national dress he was outstanding—Hollywood's idea of a sheikh. Rich Arab women might spend a fortune dressing up to look like the rich did everywhere—but the men still preferred the long flowing robes of the dashdasha when they were at home. By not needing to Westernise their appearance they not only showed how much more emancipated they were, but also set themselves physically and mentally apart from their womenfolk—and proved what superior beings they were. Well, Khalid was running true to form.

He looked up and their eyes met. He allowed his to roam slowly over her as she relaxed against the turquoise cushions of the wicker couch. She knew that with her blonde hair tumbling loosely over her shoulders and the thin cotton of her tee-shirt outlining the fullness of her breasts, she made an alluring picture. Even so she was irritated by the long appraisal to which he subjected her.

'It's rude to stare,' she stated coldly.

'I like looking at beauty.' He came across to her, drink in hand. 'Anyway, you should be used to it. Don't Englishmen stare at you?'

'Not in the same way.'

'Indeed? Are Englishmen different from other men?'

'No,' she said sweetly. 'But they're not as obvious.'

His mouth narrowed, though his lower lip still remained sensual as he handed her the drink.

'Taste this and see if it's sweet enough.'

She sipped it and nodded, and he sat beside her on the couch, one arm resting casually along the back of her cushion.

'I'm sorry I frightened you on the beach,' he said unexpectedly. 'Though I'm surprised at the way you took fright. I thought a liberated woman was above that sort of thing.'

Lorna reddened. 'In normal circumstances I'm not quite such a coward. But Dana petrified me with stories of rape and murder if I went swimming alone, and when I saw you, I panicked.'

'Serves you right for disregarding advice. I have already told you that I expect you to conform to our way of life while you are our guest here.'

Feeling she deserved the reprimand, she did not argue.

'Dana exaggerated somewhat,' he went on. 'Though she was right to warn you. We don't like our women to flaunt themselves, and those that do are asking for trouble.'

'What about the men who cause the trouble?'

'They are also dealt with.'

His words were a chilling reminder of what might lie in store for Allan if he were caught with Dana, and she could barely suppress a shudder.

Khalid saw it and mistook the reason.

'No harm will befall you while you are in my home, Lorna. I'll go with you next time you have the urge to swim in the sea. I only attack when there's a full moon.'

He sipped his drink and she made an effort to regain her composure, seizing on the first words that came into her head.

'I thought it was against your religion to drink alcohol? I know you do when you're away from home, but——'

'I'm not a Moslem,' he interrupted smoothly. 'It was the one condition my mother laid down when she sent me here.' He saw Lorna's embarrassment, but surprisingly did not chide her for her remark. Instead he looked at her thoughtfully over the rim of his glass. 'Are you seeing your brother this evening?'

'Yes—after dinner. He isn't free until late. I hope that's all right with you?'

'You don't need to ask my permission if you want to go out. You aren't here as a servant.'

'I'm not strictly here as a guest either,' she reminded him. 'You brought me here to keep Dana company, so if you're planning to go out tonight I shall stay home with her.'

'That wasn't the reason I asked what you were doing,' he said. 'It so happens that I'm dining at home and I hoped your brother could join us. I wished to meet him. But if he's busy until late, perhaps he will come over after dinner?'

Lorna did not know what to say. The invitation would delight Dana, but the thought of sitting through an evening of pretence under Khalid's watchful gaze might prove too much of a strain for her own fraught nerves.

'Thank you for the invitation,' she lied, 'but he's introducing me to some of his friends tonight.'

'Then how about tomorrow?'

'He doesn't have much free time at the moment. His department is short-staffed.'

Dark brows drew together and Lorna wondered nervously if Khalid suspected anything. Because of this, his next question came as a surprise.

'Then he won't be able to spare much time to show you around?'

'He has lots of bachelor friends who will oblige.'

'What about *my* services? I will make an excellent guide.'

Lorna hesitated. Her heart wanted her to accept the offer, but her head told her it would be unwise. Yet having hedged over accepting an invitation for Allan, she was worried that if she said no to him, it would arouse his ire. The thought of remaining in his home and having him antagonistic towards her was more than she could bear. Things would be difficult enough for her—trying to keep some control going between Dana and Allan—without adding to the danger of her position by having Khalid angry and watchful over her.

'Thank you,' she said slowly. 'I would like you to show me your country. But is it wise for us to be seen out alone? I'd hate to be responsible for ruining your reputation.'

'It's only our *women* who need to worry about their reputations—as you very well know,' he responded evenly, refusing to be drawn. 'But with your pale skin and golden hair there's no chance of anyone mistaking your origins.' He leaned forward and gently lifted a lock of her hair, letting his hand brush her cheek as he did so. 'The colour reminds me of sun-ripened corn in a Van Gogh landscape, but it's as soft to the touch as your skin against mine.' He twisted another strand around in his hand, using it to pull her face closer to his. 'I never tire of looking at you, Lorna. The more I see you, the more I want to see.'

Once more her fear of him returned. Almost from their first meeting she had fought against his magnetism, and his nearness made her tremble. His features blurred in front of her and she saw only the piercing blueness of his eyes as they gazed into her own. The blood pulsed through her body, making her conscious of every fibre.

'A nurse blushing?' he whispered. 'I don't believe it.'

Instantly her hands fluttered to her burning face. Khalid was the only man who made her feel so vulnerable, and she was alert to the danger of it. She dared not lose her control. If she did he would move in swiftly. She shifted along the couch, so that he was forced to relinquish his hold on her.

'Your eloquence took me by surprise,' she excused herself with a shaky laugh. 'Englishmen are more prosaic with their compliments.'

'And with their lovemaking too, I believe.'

With a sudden, sure movement he pulled her back across the couch and into his arms.

His mouth bore down on hers and she closed her eyes. Unable to stop herself, she found her limbs moulding themselves against his. Expecting ruthlessness, she was amazed by the gentleness of his hands and the softness of his lips. She did not want to respond, but she could not help herself, and her own lips parted.

'Golden girl,' he murmured against them. 'You are everything I've dreamed of. If only——'

'There's a messenger here from. . . .' Dana's voice trailed off as she came into the room and saw them close together.

Khalid released Lorna abruptly and stood up. 'What messenger?'

'From the office. He has some documents that need your signature.'

Without a backward glance Khalid strode out, his white robe flowing behind him.

'I'm glad you two are getting on better,' Dana commented straightfaced, as soon as he was out of earshot.

'Don't read too much into a kiss,' said Lorna. 'We were both carried away.'

'My brother doesn't get carried away easily, even by a beautiful girl. There have been too many of them.'

'Then I am just one more,' said Lorna, determined to keep things casual.

'No, you're not,' Dana denied. 'Khalid would never impugn your honour while you are a guest in his home. I think he's falling in love with you.'

Lorna brushed the suggestion aside, though her heart jumped at the words. 'Your brother would never allow himself to love a Western woman. You told me so yourself.'

'That was before I saw the effect you had on him. I know Khalid, and his behaviour towards you is quite different from normal.'

'I should hope so—we're always arguing!'

'That's why I think his interest in you is different from the others,' Dana stated triumphantly. 'If he only saw you as a pretty face he wouldn't tolerate your disagreeable nature.'

'Thanks for those kind words!'

Dana giggled like a schoolgirl. 'You know what I mean. If my brother didn't enjoy arguing with you, he wouldn't do it. He'd just ignore you completely.' The brown eyes were bright with curiosity. 'Do you love *him*?'

'Oh, for heaven's sake!' Lorna replied crossly. 'You talk too freely about love. It doesn't happen overnight, and certainly not between two people as opposite as your brother and I.'

Even as she spoke, Lorna realised there was some truth in Dana's assertion. But what she felt for Khalid was too tentative for her to be sure. Wanting a man physically did not imply love. She needed to sort out her feelings, and until she did, she would keep them to herself.

'If Khalid broke his own rules and married a Westerner,' Dana continued, 'he might change his mind about not allowing me to divorce Hassan.'

'Since he isn't likely to break his own rules,

you're indulging in daydreams. Khalid may be attracted to me, but to talk of marriage is wishful thinking.' Lorna went to the archway. 'I think I'll have a rest. What time is dinner?'

'Eight-thirty.' Dana put out her hands. 'You're not cross with me, are you?'

'No—of course not.'

Any anger Lorna felt was directed against herself for being so susceptible to Khalid. She resented everything he stood for, yet in spite of it she behaved like a child in his presence. The quicker Allan introduced her to some other men the better for her peace of mind.

Madam al Hashib joined them for dinner, and to Lorna's disappointment, the food was more French than Oriental.

'This is delicious,' she remarked, over the crab soufflé. 'But I expected something more traditional—like stuffed vine leaves.'

Madam looked at her children expectantly, and Khalid translated Lorna's comment to her. She replied swiftly in Arabic, with a warm smile directed at Lorna.

'My mother says you must dine with her one evening if you wish to taste true Eastern cooking. I find highly spiced foods disagreeable,' he explained. 'That is why the next course is roast lamb instead of kebabs.'

But Lorna did notice that in true Eastern tradition he had a very sweet tooth. In spite of the rich dessert of crème brulée, he downed several butterfly-shaped pastries that were served with the Turkish coffee. His mother murmured something to him, and he laughed. 'My mother tells me I will grow as plump as a pigeon if I continue to indulge myself,' he repeated for Lorna's benefit. 'But I have a weakness for derbils.' He proffered the sticky pastries to Lorna, but she smiled a refusal.

'Do have one,' Dana enjoined her. 'As you never put on an ounce you can afford to eat what you like. I don't eat anywhere near as much as you, but I still put on weight. I'm afraid I've inherited Mother's figure.'

'But not her disposition,' her brother teased. 'I hear you've already quarrelled with your in-laws.'

'They didn't waste much time reporting back to you,' she answered sulkily.

'Mr Rashid telephoned me. He was very upset.' Khalid frowned. 'It's only natural that they should want to see as much of Amina as possible while you're here, and by rights you *should* stay in their home.'

'Can you see Lorna being happy there?'

'I'm sure Lorna wouldn't mind where she stayed.' His eyes rested on the corn-bright hair before he spoke to his sister again. 'Since her brother appears to be tied up at the hospital, I have offered to show her the sights.'

'Lorna is here as my companion, not yours,' Dana said instantly. 'If she wants to go out, she can come with *me*.'

'Two women do not go out sightseeing alone,' he said coldly. 'As to your parents-in-law, if you wish to upset them, that is your own affair. I won't tell you what to do.'

Dana looked about to make some rude retort,

but a warning look from Lorna restrained her, and she gave an apologetic smile at her friend.

'Of course there's no need for you to stay with me the whole time. I'm sure my brother will make an interesting guide. He knows our country inside out and its history—such as it is.'

'Now I have my sister's permission, how about our going out tomorrow afternoon?' Khalid suggested. 'I have to go to the office in the morning, but I can be back by two.'

Wanting to show she was not his to command so easily, Lorna said: 'I'd like to check with Allan first. He may have made some arrangements for me.'

'He can always change them,' Khalid said haughtily. 'But don't forget to ask him if he will join us for dinner in the evening. I have invited a few friends over to celebrate Dana's return.'

'I'll speak to him and let you know in the morning.'

She was aware of Dana's eyes lighting up with pleasure at the prospect of seeing him for an entire evening, and hoped Khalid did not notice. As long as he had no reason to doubt his sister's motivation for returning to Kuwait, he would not watch her with suspicion. But if he suspected her of deception, he would observe her like a hawk, and even send her back to England.

After dinner, Lorna put on a jacket and went into the hall to wait for the car and chauffeur that was to take her to her brother's apartment, Khalid having made it clear that no woman in his household went out alone, no matter what her nationality. She was still by the door when he came into the hall, and one look at his face told her he was still angered by her rebuff of him at the dinner-table.

'Why did you make an excuse not to come sightseeing with me?' he demanded.

'It wasn't an excuse,' she lied. 'But Allan may be expecting me to go with him.'

'Since when does a brother monopolise the attention of his sister to the exclusion of other men? That's a Western custom I have not yet encountered.'

'You know very well it's got nothing to do with custom.'

Lorna did not want to look at the man standing so close to her, but she was scared that if she didn't, he would guess how much his nearness affected her. And it was his effect on her that made her decide she dared not see too much of him.

'I appreciate your desire to entertain me,' she continued. 'But I think it will be better for us both if our friendship doesn't progress any further.'

'It hasn't progressed at all,' he exclaimed. 'How can it, when you keep me at arm's length all the time?'

'What do you want me to do?' she demanded. 'Pull you into them?'

'If only you would.' His voice caressed her like a touch, and she shivered and drew a step away from him.

'Don't flirt with me, Khalid. I'm not one of your girl-friends.'

'I know.'

'Nor do I intend to become one.'

'Why not? You are not impervious to me, Lorna, so don't pretend otherwise. You are as aware of me as I am of you.'

'I'm not interested in having an affair,' she stated. 'Although I know virginity is a virtue you only appreciate in women from your own country, I nevertheless happen to be an old-fashioned girl.'

His mouth opened and then closed tightly, as if he had thought better of what he was about to say. Before he could think of something else, she heard the purr of a limousine and knew that the chauffeur was waiting for her outside the front door.

'Goodnight, Khalid,' she said quietly, and hurried down the steps.

She was trembling from her confrontation with him, but was glad he had come in search of her. At least it had given her the opportunity to make it quite clear how she felt towards him. She could only pray that from now on he would leave her alone.

Allan was waiting for her at the lift doors outside his apartment.

'I was worried about you. Everything all right?' he asked anxiously.

'Of course. We were just late starting dinner.'

He looked relieved. 'Everyone's dying to meet you,' he said, and led her into the spacious, open-plan living-room where a party of his friends were gathered.

They were predominantly English, and none of them appeared likely to reduce her to the state of blithering idiocy that Khalid seemed able to do.

As a new female on the scene, Lorna was immediately the centre of attraction, and a succession of young men were eager to date her up for as long as she remained in Kuwait.

But she carefully refused to commit herself, and it wasn't until half-way through the evening, when several more people arrived, that she thought she had met someone who might take her mind off Khalid. Neil Tennant was a fellow surgeon of Allan's, and was a ruggedly good-looking Australian.

'How about having dinner with me tomorrow night?' he asked.

'May I take a rain check on that? The al Hashibs are giving a dinner party and I've promised Khalid I'll be there.'

She sensed rather than felt Neil's shock, although he kept his voice casual as he said: 'Are you a special friend of Khalid al Hashib's?'

'Not in the way you mean,' she smiled. 'But I *am* a special friend of his sister, Mrs Rashid.'

Neil relaxed again. 'Sorry about that. But so many Western girls come out here with their eyes on the main chance that. . . .'

She half smiled. 'I gather you don't approve?'

'Not for any moral reason—when affection is involved. But it sickens me to see so many girls happy to sell themselves.'

'The men should sicken you too,' she said with asperity.

'Well, they don't. I guess I've got the same double standards as the rest of the men here. But at least I admit it.' He eyed her intently. 'I suppose you met the al Hashibs through Allan? Dana used to do voluntary work at the hospital before she had her baby. That's where I met her too.'

'Allan had nothing to do with my meeting her. One of the nurses where I worked in London introduced us.'

Lorna watched Neil's expression carefully, wondering if he suspected any relationship between Dana and Allan. But when he next spoke it was to ask if she would see him on the first night she was free.

It was not until she was leaving Allan's apartment to return home that she had the chance of telling him that Khalid had invited him to dine with them the following evening.

'I suppose I should refuse,' he said. 'But I haven't the strength of mind to do so.'

'It would look suspicious anyway. Though I don't think you should make a habit of coming over.'

'I won't do anything foolish, Lorna.'

'You mean you *hope* you won't. The best of intentions aren't always carried out.'

'I know,' he sighed. 'If only Dana could be persuaded to return to England until my contract expires, it would be far better for my peace of mind.'

And far better for mine too, Lorna thought wryly as she climbed into the car that was taking her back to the villa. The longer she stayed in Khalid's home, the more memories she would

store up and the longer it would take her to forget
him.

By the time she reached the villa it was nearly
two o'clock, and the house was in darkness. With
a feeling of relief she crossed the gardens and
entered the sanctuary of her bedroom. She had
been afraid Dana would wait up for her to discuss
Allan, and she had had her fill on that subject for
one day.

After undressing, she slipped a negligee over
her satin nightdress, then slid back the French
windows and stepped out on to the stone balcony,
hoping the cool night air would clear her mind
and enable her to view things more clearly.

Leaning on the wrought-iron balustrade that
ran the full length of the back of the villa, she
gazed out over the moonlit ocean. The waves were
dappled into froths of spun silver as they lazily
lapped the shore, while the silence was unbroken
save for the sound of the breakers.

If only her mind were as tranquil as the scene!
Barely a month ago it *had* been. Then, she had
looked forward to a reasonably uncomplicated
life—perhaps married to David or someone
equally suitable. But since Khalid had come upon
the scene he had made every other man seem dull.

Allan's friends, whom she had met tonight, had
far more in common with her, yet she had had to
force herself to appear interested in them. Their
gentle raillery had contrasted sharply with Khalid's constant sparring, and every moment away
from him had seemed a wasted one.

She shivered at the memory of this afternoon

when he had held her in his arms. Had his kisses
only been prompted by lust? The thought was so
painful that she turned sharply, intent on returning to her bedroom before the beauty of the night
made her too emotional. In the wide glass doors
she glimpsed her reflection, virginal, pale and
slender. A golden nymph whose colouring and
untouched quality would undoubtedly appeal to a
man of Khalid's temperament.

But she didn't want to appeal to him in one
way only. She wanted more. To give him more
and to take more. She put her hands to her cheeks,
dismayed at the emotion coursing through her.

'I love him,' she whispered aloud. 'I'm out of
my mind, but I love him.'

In the quiet of her room she said the words
again and tried to think what it was about Khalid
that inspired them. He was good looking and sexu-
ally attracted her. But surely that wasn't enough
to make her love him? He was intelligent, of
course, but then so were many other men she had
met. Yet none of them had the ability to look at
her and make her feel as if her bones were melting.

Perhaps love was a virus, she thought ironically,
and perhaps like a virus it would die if it had
nothing on which to feed.

The most sensible thing for her was to return to
England, but until the future of Allan and Dana
was settled, that was impossible. She frowned. She
must learn to live close to Khalid, in the intimate
atmosphere of his house, without letting him
guess the way she felt about him. It would be
difficult, but she had no other choice.

CHAPTER SEVEN

LORNA stood in front of the mirror in her bedroom and held up first one sundress and then another in an effort to decide which was more suitable for today's luncheon party: the lilac which brought out the colour of her eyes, or the acid yellow which emphasised her golden tan.

With a sigh of dissatisfaction she rummaged through the wardrobe again, hoping Neil would appreciate the effort she was making to look her best, yet knowing deep down that she was only dressing for Khalid.

She had been in Kuwait for three weeks and had managed to avoid him for the best part of them. After the welcome home dinner for Dana, which had passed off with less of a strain than she had anticipated—in spite of Allan's presence—Khalid had rarely dined at home. When he did, there were always guests present, and Lorna made sure she was safely in her room before they left.

But today he was giving a barbecue luncheon by the pool and the party was to go on until the evening. He had invited Allan, and also asked him to bring any of his friends who cared to come along —hence Neil's presence. This was typical of

Kuwaiti hospitality—at least among those who were emancipated enough to allow mixed gatherings. With money no object and countless servants to do the work, entertaining was no problem and new faces were particularly welcome.

The only cultural outlet was television, and every home boasted several sets. But it was scorned by most of the jet-setters—although it was an addiction of their elderly, less sophisticated parents. As for the cinema, anyone of any worth had their own, and it was possible to hire all the latest films. Khalid had a luxurious one below the house, where there was also a gymnasium, sauna and indoor swimming pool for refreshing dips in the winter, when it was too wet or windy to swim outside.

Dana had managed to see Allan nearly every day. Their meetings, through careful manoeuvring, were above suspicion, but it still imposed a considerable strain on Lorna, particularly when Allan came to the house, for she was always afraid Khalid's eagle eyes would notice something strange.

There had been talk of Hassan coming out to visit his wife, but fortunately that complication had not materialised.

Lorna sighed heavily. Today was not going to be enjoyable; she was certain of that. Even if she managed to avoid Khalid, she would still be seeing him, and it would put a terrible strain on her.

She was still shattered by the knowledge that she loved him, but had hoped that the futility of the situation would help her to develop an im-

munity, and even a certain numbness to his presence. But this had been wishful thinking. She still
ached for him and he was never far from her
thoughts, day or night.

Closing her mind to him as best she could, she
stepped into a rose pink dress that accentuated her
golden tan, ran a comb through her hair, which
the sun had streaked with silver glints, and walked
out of the safety of her room.

A large crowd was gathered around the pool
and several guests were swimming, though no
Kuwaitis were among them. Although emancipated enough to attend mixed gatherings, few of
them had the courage to carry their flaunting of
traditions any further. Lorna had noticed a certain unease among some of the men and women
whom she met, as if they were still not sure they
were doing the right thing. One always felt they
were looking guiltily over their shoulders, like
naughty children fearful of being caught misbe-
having by their parents.

Khalid was not among the bathers and she spotted him talking to some Westerners at the far side
of the pool. His tall figure, clad in the stark white
dashdasha that made his skin glow like bronze,
stood out among his shorter compatriots. Not that
he wouldn't have stood out in any company. Today he was not wearing his headdress, and Lorna
noticed that in the last few weeks he had let his
hair grow longer, so that it curled over the high
collar of his robe and made him look younger.

He looked up unexpectedly and their eyes met.
For an instant he was motionless, then he threaded

his way towards her, the springiness of his step and his air of alertness reminding her of a sleek black panther. He closed in on her with a purposeful look in his eyes and again she had the impression of a big cat about to pounce on his cornered victim.

She almost turned and fled, but she forced a serene smile to her lips and hoped he had not noticed her loss of control.

'Hullo, stranger,' he said, his eyes moving from her face to her body, and back to her face again. 'Today you will not be able to avoid me.'

She gave a nervous laugh. 'I haven't been avoiding you.'

'Don't lie to me.' He kept his voice soft so that no one should hear them, but his eyes were icy. 'I'm not a fool, Lorna. You have refused to let me show you my country—even though you had originally agreed—and when I am home with you, you rush away from me like a startled deer.'

'Perhaps I feel like one,' she retorted.

'Do you see me as the stag that's hunting you?'

'Yes.'

'Then you should know that he invariably catches her.'

'Unless another stag gets her first.'

His indrawn breath was audible. 'Who is the other stag, Lorna?'

Fearing the way the conversation was going, she tried to lighten it.

'There isn't only one, Khalid. There are dozens. Allan's friends have inundated me with invitations.'

'Which you have felt compelled to accept,' he said drily. 'Or is it that you wish to make sure your time is occupied?'

'Why shouldn't I want to see you?' she asked defiantly.

'I'll answer that question when we are alone. For the moment I have left my American guests unattended. Come, I wish you to meet them.'

It was a command rather than a request, and to make sure she did not disobey it he caught her hand and tucked it firmly into his arm. She felt the hard muscles of his ribs as he pressed his elbow tightly against his chest, and had to resist the urge to move her fingers over them.

'This is Ellen and Bob Driver,' he said, as they reached the couple to whom he had been speaking earlier. They were both tall, with sandy-coloured hair, and looked to be in their late thirties. 'Bob is my American lawyer and has come here for two months to drum up business with my competitors.'

'Don't kid this lovely lady,' the tall, bespectacled American replied with a strong Southern accent. 'You're too dog-in-the-manger to let me represent anyone other than you.'

Lorna wondered if this attitude of Khalid's also applied to the women in his life, and wished she could see him with one of them. Though Dana frequently spoke of her brother's love affairs, he had been the soul of discretion here. Yet she did not believe he had remained celibate all these weeks; his masculinity was too strong. It was all too easy to picture him with a woman, his bronzed body lying upon a slender one, his lips seeking out all the intimate places of desire. She trembled at the thought and resolutely pushed it aside as Ellen spoke to her.

'How long are you staying in Kuwait?'

'I'm not quite sure.'

'Do you like it?'

Lorna made herself concentrate on the question, but was still painfully aware of Khalid standing close to her. It was a relief when he saw some other guests and moved over to greet them, taking Bob Driver with him.

Left alone, the two women settled themselves on one of the gaily patterned hammocks that dotted the side of the pool. The American had the usual easy-going warmth of her countrywomen, and it was not long before she knew Lorna's life-story.

Khalid was now standing near the buffet, which was directly opposite where the two girls were sitting, and Lorna was so conscious of his gaze upon her that it was obvious that *his* mind was not on any business discussion. Ellen's pale grey eyes noticed it too, and she wasted no time in coming to the point.

'Have you two got something going?' she asked.

Normally Lorna would never have confided in a stranger, but she felt the same instinctive warmth towards Ellen that she had felt when first meeting Dana. It was as if they were already old friends.

'What makes you think that?' she parried with a small smile.

'I felt the vibes when you came up to us.' She

appraised Lorna frankly. 'You're a great looking girl and he's the most dishy man I know. And single. So what's the problem?'

'I'm an old-fashioned girl. I don't just want to be his girl-friend.'

Ellen looked sympathetic. 'Face up to it, honey; I doubt if you could be anything more. I know Khalid fairly well. He and Bob have been associated for a number of years, and their fathers did business together before that, so I've heard his views on women all too often. They make my blood boil,' she continued, 'but I keep my mouth shut. Khalid's a great guy, but he likes women to know their place.'

'Unfortunately it isn't where I'd want *my* place to be,' Lorna stated.

'So how come you're staying here? The longer you do, the harder it will be for you to forget him.'

'I know. But I can't let Dana down. She—she hasn't been well and I want to stay with her until she's better.'

Ellen looked surprised. 'I saw her with a doctor from the hospital soon after we arrived and I thought she looked great.'

Lorna swallowed hard and tried not to show her consternation.

'That must have been my brother. He and Dana have known each other for ages. She used to do voluntary work at the hospital where he works.'

Ellen looked about to say more, and in an effort to distract her, Lorna pretended to have a fit of coughing. It developed into a genuine bout as she saw Allan and Dana coming towards them.

For the first time she noticed that Dana did indeed look blooming. Living at such close quarters with her and very much absorbed with her own problems, she had not noticed the change. Now she could not avoid seeing it, and feared that others had noticed it too.

'Neil's been looking everywhere for you.' Allan bent to kiss his sister. 'I'll go and bring him across.'

'I will have a servant do it.' Khalid had silently glided up to join them. 'I would be desolate to think that Lorna's day was spoiled because she did not have the partner of her choice at her side.' His voice was level but his gaze was blue fire as it rested on Lorna and then focused on Ellen. 'You may be the belle of the South, my dear Ellen,' he went on gallantly, 'but Lorna is the belle of the East.'

'Is she the belle in your life too?' Ellen asked with a mischievous grin.

'Naturally. I love all beautiful women—and Lorna is outstandingly so.'

Unable to take any more, Lorna stood up. 'Don't bother looking for Neil. I'll take a stroll and find him for myself.'

'Not until you have eaten.'

Khalid barred her way, making it impossible for her to move without brushing him aside. Knowing that if she touched him she would be lost, she acquiesced and followed him to the buffet.

She was not hungry and Khalid's presence robbed her of what little appetite she had. But she drank liberally in an effort to blot out his presence.

Khalid stuck to orange juice, maintaining his refusal to drink spirits in front of anyone other than his immediate family. For some reason this now annoyed her.

'As you're not a Moslem,' she said waspishly, 'I can't see why you stick to fruit juice. You don't strike me as the sort of man to care what your friends think.'

'I do it as a sign of respect to my father's memory.'

'I'm surprised you didn't become a Moslem, then.'

'I toyed with the idea,' he admitted. 'When my father was alive I discussed it with him many times, but for some reason that I still cannot fathom, he was very much against it.'

'What will happen if you marry a Muslim girl?' she asked, flagellating herself at the thought of him with a wife.

'I'll wait until that happens and then decide.'

She blinked rapidly to hide the tears that pricked the back of her eyes, and forced herself to concentrate on the small band of gypsy violinists who were playing on a dais at the far side of the pool.

'I didn't know you had gypsies in Kuwait,' she said.

'We don't. They are foreign labourers who earn extra money this way.'

'Are those labourers too?' she enquired, pointing to a group of musicians in white dinner jackets who were also making their way to the dais.

'I think you've had too much champagne,'

Khalid told her gently. 'Otherwise I'm sure you'd recognise them. They're one of Las Vegas' leading cabaret acts. I brought them over for the party.'

Such a high-handed use of wealth only served to increase the barriers between them, and her misery intensified, making her sharp with him.

'Forgive my ignorance, Khalid, but Las Vegas isn't on my itinerary. Until I came here I'd never travelled outside Europe.'

'That's a shame, my beautiful Lorna. The world should be your oyster.'

'I don't like oysters,' she retorted. 'However, I'm very impressed by your affluence.'

'I didn't do it to impress you. Why do you always misinterpret my actions?'

'I wasn't aware I did. Please accept my humblest apologies if I've upset you.'

'You are still upsetting me.' Anger had paled his tan. 'You give me no chance to show you that I am not the man you first met in London.'

'Leopards don't change their spots. They may learn to disguise them—that's all.'

His eyes blazed at her, blue as the sea that glittered in the distance behind him.

'You know nothing about me,' he grated.

'And you know nothing about me. If you did, you would stop pestering me and realise I mean what I say. I'm not looking for a lover, Khalid. When I give myself to a man, he will be my husband.'

He leaned close, his body masking her from the people around them.

'Then you admit you have thought of me as your lover?'

Knowing she had boxed herself into a corner, she looked for a way out. 'You're a stunning looking man, Khalid. Most girls would think of you like that. Now would you kindly go away and leave me alone. Everyone is looking at us.'

'So what?'

'So they'll think we *are* having an affair.'

'I don't give a damn what anyone thinks.'

'But I do.' Annoyance helped her to stand up to him. 'Obviously you don't give a damn what you do to my reputation. After all, I'm not a Kuwaiti and——'

'Shut up!' he hissed, and catching her by the elbow, pulled her fast towards the house.

She tried to resist, but short of an undignified struggle there was no choice but to obey him. Her head swam as she moved, and she realised she had drunk too much champagne.

'You need some strong black coffee,' Khalid said as they reached the cool atmosphere of the hall. 'Go to your room and I'll bring it to you.'

'What are your servants here for?' she replied tartly. 'Or do you think I'm too sozzled to stop you taking advantage of me?'

'I have never needed to take advantage of any woman,' he stated matter-of-factly. 'I find they are only too happy to give themselves to me.'

'Well, this is one who won't. So leave me alone!'

With a toss of her head she went to her room.

Her head was aching and her eyelids felt leaden. Love and pain mingled inside her and she lay on the bed and wished herself back in England; back in time to the days before Khalid had come into her life. Khalid. . . . She buried her face in the pillow.

When she awoke the soft shadows of approaching evening provided a welcome relief from the harsh daylight. She was pleased to find her headache had gone and she raised her head slightly to gaze out of the window, watching the blue sky swiftly turn cobalt, tinged with purple and red.

'Beautiful, isn't it?' a deep voice said.

With a gasp she sat up higher and saw Khalid in the armchair on the other side of her bed.

'What are you . . . you haven't been here all this time, have you?'

'No. If I had, my friends' suspicions would have turned into certainty. But I've been coming in from time to time to see how you were.'

He rose and switched on the bedside lamp. It threw a warm pink glow over the room and disclosed the thermos flask and cup on the ivory inlaid table.

'Coffee,' he said, filling the cup for her. 'It will refresh you. When you've finished it I hope you will feel well enough to join us again.'

Lorna wondered what he would say if she said she would prefer to stay here alone with him, and knew that even to hint such a thing would be to burn her boats irrevocably.

'I'll rest for a bit longer and then come out.

There's no need for you to wait here with me,' she told him.

'I enjoy being here.'

'Without regard for my good name, of course,' she said bitterly.

'You have no cause to say that. If I didn't have a conscience about you, I'd have set out to seduce you weeks ago.'

She glared at him, almost speechless, but not quite. 'You've got a hell of a nerve!'

'Because I'm being honest with you? Do you want me to be dishonest and say I haven't lain awake at night aching to have you? That I haven't wanted to come into your room and possess your warmth and softness?'

'You wouldn't have found me warm and soft for long,' she flared.

Humour glittered in his eyes and it intensified her temper.

'If you won't promise to leave me alone, Khalid, I'll move in with Allan,' she threatened.

Instantly the humour vanished. 'You will what?'

'You heard me. I know I promised to stay with Dana for as long as she needs me, but I can do that just as easily if I live with my brother.'

'You are not to leave my home,' he ordered. 'You will stay here for ever.'

She was not sure she had heard him correctly, and seeing her expression, Khalid moved closer to the bed, only stopping as she drew back in fright.

'Don't be scared of me,' he said quietly, 'I will

never harm you. But I want you to remain in my home for ever.'

'I can't.' Lorna was conscious of panic. 'Please, Khalid, stay away from me.'

'As my wife,' he went on softly, ignoring her interruption.

Lorna was positive she was dreaming. She pressed her nails into her palms to wake herself up, but though she winced with the pain, the scene did not change and Khalid remained at the foot of her bed, dark as a panther, watchful as an eagle.

'If this is your idea of a joke——' she whispered.

'A joke!' he echoed, his voice anguished. 'It's more like a torment! If you knew how much I have fought against my feelings for you. . . . But I can't fight any longer. You've got to marry me, Lorna. I won't take no for an answer.'

She went on staring at him, wondering why she was not overjoyed by what he had said. Perhaps it was because he had not used the word 'love'. Yes, that was why she felt fear instead of pleasure. He wanted her; he longed to possess her and submit her to his will. But he did not love her.

'Have you nothing to say?' he asked huskily, and came closer.

He bent towards her, but he did not attempt to take her in his arms, and there was a rigidity about his stance that clearly showed the effort he was making not to do so.

'It won't work, Khalid,' she said.

'It will. If you want me as much as I want you. . . .'

'How long will the wanting last?'

His brows drew together in a dark silky line above his firm nose. 'What do you mean?'

'How long do your affairs usually last?' she asked coldly.

'What has that got to do with my proposal? I want you for my wife, not my girl-friend. Isn't that what you want too? You can't tell me I've imagined the way you feel?'

'No,' she admitted. 'But that still doesn't mean I can marry you.' She drew a deep breath, then forced herself to continue. 'If I'd given in to you —if I'd been willing to go to bed with you, you would never have proposed marriage. You're only doing it now because your passion is stronger than your convictions.'

He stared at her. His features were taut in the lamplight, his eyes looked dark, making him seem more foreign, so that it was easy to visualise him only as his father's son, a product of a totally alien culture. Then he moved, and Lorna saw the gleam of blue irises and was reminded that for all his denial, his mother was British as she herself was.

'I deserve your accusation,' Khalid said slowly. 'I don't know how my feelings would have developed if you had given in to me. All I can say is that I would not have grown tired of you. It is quite possible that even after you had become my mistress I would still have wanted to marry you.'

'Thanks!'

'I am being serious, Lorna. Don't be sarcastic. My feelings for you go deeper than sexual attraction, although admittedly that was my original motivation. And I certainly wanted to make you submit to me.' His mouth quirked. 'You are the only woman who has ever argued with me, and my first reaction was not to give you a second thought. But I found I couldn't *stop* thinking about you. I even enjoyed our fights. Nor did I resent the fact that your opinions were so different from my own. It was then that I realised I loved you as a person and not as a possession.' He put up his hand and raked his fingers through his hair. 'I've never regarded a woman in that way before, and it was something I found hard to understand.'

'You hid your feelings well,' she said, still unable to believe all he had just told her.

'They were so new to me that I needed time to absorb them. But now I have, and I know I'll never be satisfied with a wife who is a mere puppet. I will frequently find you maddening, but I will always find you adorable. You are the only woman I. . . .' He paused, met her eyes and said: 'I love you, Lorna. I love you with all my heart; with all the breath in my body.'

With a soft cry she held out her hands and with an answering cry he closed his arms around her. For an instant she held back, then she abandoned herself to the magic of his touch.

His sensuous, hungry lips found hers, and the hardening of his body told her how strong his desire was. Her own desire rose to meet it, and her limbs became soft and pliant, melting against him, aching for them to be one as his mouth trailed over the soft skin of her cheeks to find the hollow of her neck and then slid down to her breasts.

'Darling,' he said thickly, and buried his face against them, his lips caressing the satin curves until she trembled at the sensations he aroused in her.

Lifted to undreamed-of heights, Lorna felt as if nothing could assuage the longing she felt for this man. Her fear of him died, as did her need to keep him at arm's length, and as he went to pull back she drew his head down again.

'Don't go yet, Khalid. Stay a bit longer.'

'I daren't. If I do, I won't be responsible for my actions.'

'Then let me take the responsibility.'

He chuckled, though it was also partly a groan as he drew her hands down to her sides and sat up straight. But he remained beside the bed, looking down at her as she lay on the pillows, her hair splayed out in golden abandon.

'You are aware of my deep passions,' he said quietly. 'I will not deny I'm a man who enjoys sex and wants it frequently. That's why we got off to such a bad start. But because we did, I will not let you seduce me into forgetting the vow I made while I watched you sleeping.'

'What vow?' she asked.

'To wait until you are my wife before making you my woman.'

'Khalid, I. . . .'

Foolish tears flowed and, seeing them, he pulled her up into his arms again, stroking her hair and murmuring tender nothings into her ear.

'I'm so happy,' she cried. 'I can't believe this isn't a dream from which I'll wake up.'

'Pray God that neither of us will wake up from this dream.' He pressed his lips to the damp waves that curled across her forehead. 'Let us go and tell my stepmother our news. Once she knows, I shall be able to tell my friends.' His eyes gleamed. 'We can announce it this evening.'

'So soon?' She drew back and the movement made her aware of her naked breasts. Hurriedly she snatched at the bodice of her dress to cover them.

His smile widened. 'Aren't you used to the human form, Nurse Lorna?'

'Not in these particular circumstances,' she smiled back at him. 'If you were ill and I had to look after you, I'd think nothing of it. But that's quite different from having you sit beside me like this.'

'It certainly is,' he said wryly. 'Which makes me all the more convinced that I can't wait long to make you my wife.'

A sudden doubt assailed her. Was Khalid afraid that if he waited to announce their marriage he might lose his nerve? After all, he had always professed himself a traditionalist, and his choice of a Western bride might appear as a betrayal of all his beliefs.

'I won't change my mind about you,' he said, as if he had read her thoughts. 'I know we will have problems, but if we love each other enough, we will overcome them.'

'I wish I were as sure as you,' she said shakily.

'Be sure,' he asserted. 'Because of our differences we will have to try much harder for an understanding, and that will bring us closer together.'

'Will we always be close?' she asked. 'You travel a lot and——'

'You will travel with me until the babies come.' Colour stole into her cheeks and the sight of it moved him to gather her closer. 'When that happens, my dearest, I will curtail my travels. I have no intention of being a stay-away husband, nor of having other women. You will be everything to me, as I will be to you.'

She longed to echo his words, yet even as she tried, she found she couldn't, for implicit in them was a joint existence that would preclude her from following any life of her own.

'You have your business interests, Khalid, and they'll keep you occupied,' she said. 'But having children won't occupy all my time, particularly as we'll have so many servants.'

'Does that mean you will want to go on working?' he asked, coming straight to the point in a way which made her love him more, and also realise he was a man with whom she would rarely be able to prevaricate.

'Yes, Khalid, that's exactly what I mean.'

'Then you can. But it must be a job that will allow you to accompany me when I go abroad. There are many charitable organisations here that could do with someone like you at their head.'

It all sounded too good to be true, but Lorna

was intelligent enough to know there would be many instances when she and Khalid would quarrel on this subject. At the moment he was ready to agree to anything she asked of him, but she doubted if he would be as compliant once they were married.

'I think we should tape this conversation,' she said. 'Then you won't be able to deny you said it.'

'I could never deny you anything,' he said seriously. 'If your beauty fails to win me over, your intelligence will do it for you.'

'I could say the same about you.'

'But naturally.' His lids narrowed. 'That is what makes us so compatible.'

She laughed and he moved to the door. 'I'll go outside while you change. Don't keep me waiting too long.'

She smiled and blew him a kiss, knowing she had already kept him waiting longer than any other woman had done.

The news of Khalid's engagement did not seem to come as a surprise to his stepmother. She embraced him warmly, but was more reserved towards Lorna.

'You make Khalid happy, then ... I ... happy,' she said falteringly.

Lorna hoped this would also be the reaction of Khalid's friends, though she doubted it, and said as much to him when they left his stepmother's apartment.

'I bet all the single girls in Kuwait will want to scratch my eyes out! You're probably one of the most eligible men in the country and you're being snapped up by a foreigner.'

'Not being,' he corrected, 'but been. As soon as I saw you without your disguise, my defences crumbled. I put up a fight, but it was a losing battle.'

She did not like to think of Khalid trying so hard not to love her, but remembering how unhappy his father's marriage to an Englishwoman had been, she could understand it.

'I'll never knowingly let you down,' she avowed.

'Nor I you. Everything I am and everything I have is yours.'

'I'm only interested in the man,' she smiled. 'To be honest, I find your wealth overwhelming.'

'You'll soon get used to it.' His eyes fixed approvingly on her silk crocheted dress, the same rose pink as her lips. 'The trouble is I can't see you looking more beautiful in a couture dress than you do in that cheap one.'

'It wasn't cheap for me,' she protested. 'It was more expensive than I could afford.'

'From now on you can afford everything your heart desires, and it will be my pleasure to give it to you.'

The thought that all this implied frightened her. But she did not say so, knowing he would not understand her reaction.

He caught her hand and drew it to his lips. 'Let us rejoin my friends and announce our news.'

Before she could tell him she wanted to speak to her brother alone first, he pulled her across the

marble hall to the huge salon, and within moments they were surrounded by well-wishers. She
saw the stunned amazement on Allan's face and
the incredulous joy on Dana's, and knew that both
of them were wondering what this augured for
their own chance of finding happiness together.

Indeed Allan had less pleasant thoughts on the
matter, and getting her alone in a corner, bluntly
asked if she genuinely loved Khalid or was
stringing him along in the hope of persuading him
to let Dana have her freedom.

'Do you really think I'd hurt Khalid by doing
such a thing?' she asked, amazed. 'I may be a
loving sister, but I'm not a heartless bitch.'

Allan sighed. 'Sorry, old girl, but I had to be
sure.' His lips tightened as he looked over to where
Khalid was receiving more congratulations. 'I
don't know what sort of a husband he'll make
you, but I'm damn sure he'd be a bitter enemy.
That's why I had to know how you felt about him.
I suppose you haven't given the folks a hint that
this might happen?'

'I didn't even know it myself until half an hour
ago.' A shadow deepened the violet of her eyes.
'Do you think they'll like Khalid?'

'Of course. But they'll be worried for you,
particularly if you have to live out here. You
won't have the freedom you've been used to,
Lorna. Khalid's Westernised in some ways, but
he'll still expect Arab-style obedience from you.'

Lorna shied away from this, telling herself that
Khalid was half English, and that though he was
totally Arab in outlook and tradition, once she

was his wife she would be able to change him.

Yet a short while ago she had told him that leopards didn't change their spots—and now she was trying to pretend otherwise. She sighed. Khalid had not swept away her doubts, but her longing to be his wife was so strong that she had convinced herself that nothing else mattered.

She looked at Allan. 'I wish things could work out for you and Dana.'

'I doubt if they will, Hassan won't let her stay here much longer, and once she's back with him, he'll give her another child—which will tie her to him completely.'

Lorna remained silent, unwilling to give Allan false hope. Yet she determined to tell Khalid the whole story as soon as their own relationship matured. In the light of his own happiness she felt sure he would want the same for his sister. After all, character was only partly formed by environment. Hereditary factors also played an important part in one's development, and given time her influence over Khalid would help him to see things as she did; the way he would have seen things if his parents hadn't parted.

A long time later she was to remember these hopes, and wonder how she could have been so naïve.

CHAPTER EIGHT

IN spite of her misgivings, the next six weeks were the happiest of Lorna's life. The days were not long enough, as they were swept up in a hectic round of entertainment.

The family—of which Khalid was the titular head—was enormous, and she had great difficulty in remembering which cousin was which. On the surface she appeared to be accepted by them, but she was sensitive enough to recognise that a few of them disapproved of Khalid's behaviour, however carefully they tried to hide it.

Wisely she said nothing to Khalid, unwilling for him to think she was criticising his family. Yet she could not dismiss the fear that his relatives might make him have second thoughts. However, he gave no sign of it, and within a few days of their engagement he arranged for Lorna's parents and several of her close friends to fly out for their wedding, which was to take place in a month's time. He had wanted to make it sooner, but had agreed to her plea to wait.

'We still need time to get to know each other better,' she said. 'A few extra weeks won't make any difference.'

'You wouldn't say that if you saw me pacing the floor at night,' he quipped, tracing little kisses along the side of her throat. 'It's agony having to leave you at the door of your room.'

'Do you think I don't feel the same?' she asked, burying her head against his shoulder, while the hardening of his thighs as he pressed against her set her pulses racing. She heard him sigh regretfully as he drew away from her.

'You're worth waiting for, golden girl. But if I had my way I'd marry you tomorrow.'

'If you want to make love to me,' she said huskily, 'I won't——'

'No,' he cut in. 'You will come to the altar a virgin—which is what you wish. I know how you feel about it, and I respect your desire.'

He was as good as his word and turned out to be the perfect suitor, spending as little time at his office as he could, and accompanying her everywhere, even when she shopped for her trousseau.

He delighted in lavishing expensive presents on her at every opportunity, and one afternoon met her in the foyer of the Sheraton Hotel and ushered her up to the mezzanine floor and into the Blue Room, which was opposite the hotel's mosque. It was filled with fashionably dressed young sheikhas and their husbands, all examining the exhibition of fabulous jewellery displayed there by an exclusive American store.

'I've picked out something for you,' Khalid said, 'but I want your approval before I buy it.' He stopped in front of one of the salesmen, who produced a bracelet and necklace of amethysts and diamonds in a white gold setting.

'It's lovely!' she gasped. 'But you've got to stop buying me so much.'

'Why?' He held the necklace against her throat. 'It exactly matches your eyes.'

Lorna knew he would continue to buy her presents regardless of her protests, and could appreciate why so many French and Italian fashion houses displayed their goods here. The suburb of Salamiyya might not be the Faubourg St Honoré, but their boutiques only stocked the best, and money changed hands with a rapidity that was almost shocking. What Kuwaiti women lacked in emancipation, they more than made up for in spending power.

Even Carita of Paris ran a hairdressing and beauty salon here, and Lorna was tempted to have her hair cut short. But Khalid stopped her, saying he preferred it long and loose.

'All the better for me to catch you by,' he teased.

'You won't have any need. I'll never run away.'

'I hope you will always feel like this. I want you to think of Kuwait as your home.'

Lorna doubted that she ever could. To her, the country seemed to have no soul. Very few buildings survived from the pre-oil era, and those that did were often derelict and waiting to be torn down. The Kuwaitis had a passionate belief that only new was beautiful, though most of the monotonous glass and concrete buildings that dominated the city disproved this. In fact one of the very few that deserved the description was the

Amir's Seir Palace, although having been completed at the beginning of the sixties, it was already considered an ancient monument. It was built in the heart of what was once the old part of the city, and the upper edge was topped with a castellated parapet that reminded Lorna of an old-style desert fortress.

One afternoon Khalid took her up in the lift to the clock tower of the Palace, which was crowned with a small golden dome, and they emerged on to a balcony that gave them an excellent view of the town.

'Have you ever been inside the palace itself?' Lorna asked, after admiring the panorama for a few minutes.

'Often. His Highness spends five mornings a week receiving foreign visitors and delegations, and he frequently asks me to join them. He only sees men, of course.'

'Of course,' Lorna exclaimed so meaningfully that Khalid chuckled.

'In spite of that, we are not as backward here as you think. The legal status of Kuwaiti women is the most advanced in the Gulf. They got the vote in 1975.'

'How many husbands allow them to use it? And how many women here understand what they're voting for?'

'Doesn't that apply equally to Western women? Most of them aren't interested in politics and usually echo their husband's views.'

'You never let me win, do you?' Lorna sighed, and linked her arm through his. 'Tell me more about Women's Lib Kuwaiti style.'

He looked pensive for a minute. 'There's a special ladies' department in the Kuwait National Bank. It's run by a widow of one of the bank's directors. She has an office there and women with their own bank accounts can come in to do business.'

'It still means your women are segregated. Why should they have a special department in the bank? Why can't they use the same one as the men?'

'Don't make an argument of it,' he smiled. 'In the olden days women weren't even allowed to handle any money, except for their housekeeping allowance.'

They had never discussed money matters, and Lorna wondered whether Khalid would allow her to be independent. If he only wanted her to do charity work, she would soon use up her savings.

As was so often the case, he immediately guessed her thoughts.

'I want you to be financially independent, Lorna, and I will settle some money on you so that you will have all you need for your day-to-day expenses.'

She hid a smile. Khalid's idea of day-to-day expenses was enough to satisfy the average person for three months. But she did not say so. There was likely to be plenty of things on which they would disagree, but she refused to let her pride make money one of them.

Later that afternoon they went to the exclusive Hunting and Equestrian Club. It appeared to be miles from anywhere and looked like a military base, being walled in, with its gates firmly shut on outsiders.

A blast on Khalid's horn quickly opened them, and she was delighted to find the grounds pleasantly green, especially when compared with the usual dust-bowl of concrete and desert of Kuwait.

'There's stabling for forty-seven horses, a nine-hole golf course and a skeet-shooting range,' Khalid informed her as he brought his Cadillac to a halt outside the American-style club-house.

Several of his friends—in mixed and family groups—sat on the neatly hedged lawn, and they waved and called for him to join them. But he shook his head and pointed towards the club-house.

'I've arranged to meet the Drivers here for tea,' he informed Lorna as they entered the cool of the lounge.

A large colour television set was on, but everyone was too busy gossiping to pay it any attention.

'I wish you'd told me what this place was like,' she complained, watching his eyes follow a couple of pretty girls in flowing chiffon. 'I'd have put on something smarter than a cotton dress. All the women here look as if they're going to a garden party at Buckingham Palace.'

'You look perfect whatever you wear,' he responded instantly. 'If these women were as beautiful as you, they would also get away with simplicity.'

'You and your compliments!' she sniffed.

Ignoring her comment, he drew her towards Bob and Ellen Driver who were seated in the far corner, deep in conversation with a Kuwaiti couple. Khalid knew them, and though Lorna discovered they had been at his luncheon party, she did not remember them.

Nadia and Abdulla Ladin were both English-educated and great Anglophiles. They spoke familiarly of London, where they lived for part of the year, and it made her feel so homesick that she wondered how she would adapt to the nomadic life she would lead as Khalid's wife. Their main home would be in Kuwait, but they would flit from country to country for at least half of the year. If only their permanent home could be in England! Remembering how the marriage of Khalid's parents had foundered, she was afraid even to suggest it.

The Ladins were both lawyers and had the most modern marriage of any of the couples she had met here so far. They travelled everywhere together, and though Nadia did not practise law professionally, her husband often consulted her privately.

'They seem really contented,' Lorna remarked as she and Khalid drove back to the villa. 'Theirs must have been a love match.'

'Sorry to disappoint you, darling, but Nadia only met Abdulla three times before she became his wife.' His foot came down hard on the brake as a battered old Fiat in front of them stopped abruptly, steam pouring from the bonnet. 'It's all a question of attitudes,' he continued as he overtook the hapless driver and the car picked up speed again. 'If you accept an arranged marriage as your lot, you *can* make it work. But it's no good entering into it reluctantly.'

'You mean as Dana did?' she asked boldly, and wondered if she dared tell him the truth about his sister and Allan. Keeping it a secret from him was one of the few things that marred her happiness.

Khalid frequently expressed his admiration for her honesty, and each time he did, her conscience pricked. She had to tell him soon, for she knew he would never forgive her if he learned about it from anyone else.

'We must have no secrets from each other,' he had told her not so long ago. 'You should never be frightened to confide in me. We are to be as one, in mind as well as body.'

Taking him at his word, she had questioned him about his real mother, and surprisingly he had shown none of the touchiness he had displayed when they had first met and Dana had mentioned her.

'I know you find it difficult to understand that I never want to see her,' he had confided, 'but I can't think of her as my mother. From the time I was seven, when she sent me out here, she ignored my existence. Yet my stepmother accepted me and loved me as if I were her own child.'

'And you've never seen your mother since?' Lorna asked, imagining Khalid as a little boy, and wondering how any woman could be so heartless.

He hesitated. 'I'll let you into a secret. When I was at Harvard I went to New York to see her.

She had little to say to me and was unwilling for me to meet her new husband. She was quite frank about the reason. He didn't know of my existence, and being years younger than she was, he would have been horrified to find she had a son near his own age. She had told him she was thirty-five—and truthfully she didn't look more. It's amazing what a good face-lift can do.'

'She sounds a bitch,' Lorna said flatly. 'You're lucky she didn't bring you up. A loving step-mother is much better than an unloving mother.'

Khalid had given an unexpectedly relaxed smile. 'How right you are! You're so sensible, Lorna, you help me to see things in perspective.' He caught her close. 'Perhaps you can now understand why having *your* love means so much to me?'

His statement had nearly been Lorna's undoing, and if one of his cousins had not arrived unexpectedly, she would have told him about Dana and Allan there and then. But by the time the man had gone, caution had overcome conscience, and she had held her tongue.

'I think Dana's got over that love affair in London, don't you?' Khalid's voice broke into her reverie as they drew up outside the villa. 'I've never seen her look better. I'm certain having you here has made all the difference.'

In more ways than one, Lorna thought with disquiet. Allan and Dana had been able to see considerably more of each other since her own engagement to Khalid, and Dana had even made up a foursome with Allan on some of their sightseeing forays. What could be more natural than for Lorna's brother to accompany them? It was only because Khalid believed in Lorna's integrity that he had not suspected anything.

'You're very quiet,' he commented as he helped her out of the car, kissing her swiftly on the lips before mounting the steps to the entrance. 'I hope all your thoughts have been occupied with me?'

Now was the time to tell him the truth, she decided. Khalid's uncle was giving a party for them tonight—an extravagant affair with three hundred guests. She would suggest they have a quiet drink together before they left, and she would tell him then.

Nervous at what she had to say, Lorna took longer to change than she expected, but she was anxious to look her best, hoping his anger would be lessened if he were distracted by her beauty. Until now it had never occurred to her to use it as a weapon. She had accepted her looks without realising the power they could wield; but sexual attraction played such a strong role in their relationship that she was prepared to sway Khalid by any means at her command.

Huge, worry-filled violet eyes stared back at her from the dressing-table mirror. Suppose he did not understand and blamed her for condoning Allan and Dana's behaviour? She felt a tightening in the pit of her stomach. It was foolish to take a pessimistic view. Hadn't Khalid asked her to marry him in spite of his convictions that East and West did not mix? Why shouldn't he now show the same tolerance towards his sister? It was true that

Dana's circumstances were different—after all, she was married and had a child.

The thought of Amina made Lorna frown. It was the custom here for a wife to give up her first child to her husband's mother—as a recompense for taking her son—and she knew that had it not been for Khalid's intervention, Dana would have been obliged to hand over her little girl to her mother-in-law. But Hassan might insist on this if Dana left him, and for this reason too, it was imperative to have Khalid on their side, for only he had sufficient power to enforce his own wishes.

And I've got to make him wish that Dana is free to find happiness with the man she loves, Lorna thought, and prayed for Khalid to be in a receptive mood.

One look at his face as she entered the salon told her he was not. He was paler than she had ever seen him and his eyes were like chips of blue ice.

'Darling, what's wrong?' she exclaimed, and half ran towards him.

It was only as she came further into the room that she had her answer. Dana and Allan were sitting close together on one of the settees. Their faces were strained and Dana's eyes were puffy from crying.

'I suppose you've been a party to this deception all along?' Khalid spoke with a harshness Lorna had never heard before.

'I wanted to tell you—I was going to do it tonight.' She saw the disbelief on his face and knew it was imperative to make him believe her.

'It's true, Khalid. I hated having this secret from you, but——'

'It wasn't Lorna's secret to tell,' Dana interrupted. 'She's always detested having to lie, but she did it for my sake.'

'And for her brother's too,' Khalid bit out. 'Being a member of the al Hashib family would have been quite a coup for him.'

'That remark is uncalled-for,' said Allan, and rose swiftly to his feet. 'My love for Dana has nothing to do with her position.'

'Her position as my sister, or her position as a married woman?' Khalid sneered. 'Do you know what the penalty is for adultery in this country?'

'I know there's one law for the men and one for the women.'

Afraid that if the two men went on talking like this they would come to blows, Lorna knew she had to intervene.

'Allan and Dana love each other, Khalid, the way we do.'

'Spare me your lies,' he replied roughly. 'Your brother and my sister may well feel a genuine affection for each other, but they can never have a future together.'

'By whose edict?'

'By the laws of my country.'

'By *your* laws, you mean,' she said swiftly. 'If you were willing to speak to Hassan, I'm sure he'd——'

'I refuse to be told what to do,' Khalid thundered.

'You only like to *give* orders,' Lorna snapped

back. 'But what right do you have to stop Dana from being happy?'

'She is another man's wife. That is what is right.'

'She was forced into marriage!'

'We will not discuss it any more.' He swung round on Allan. 'You must have been delighted when Lorna and I became engaged. I suppose you thought it would make it easier for you to get Dana?'

'I thought it might make you more understanding of love. Beyond that, I thought nothing.'

'Then maybe it was Lorna who did the thinking for you.'

'If you're saying my sister became engaged to you in order to help me, you must be out of your mind!' snapped Allan.

'I have indeed been out of my mind,' Khalid agreed softly.

All the anger had gone from him; both his voice and demeanour were muted, yet Lorna sensed that something dreadful had come in its place. She shivered, fearful of what was in store.

She wished with all her heart that she had found the courage to tell Khalid the truth about Dana and Allan on the day he had proposed to her. Remembering the idyllic moments they had shared together in her bedroom, she knew he would have listened in a far different frame of mind from the one he was in now. Because she understood his fury she could not blame him for his lack of belief in her good faith.

'I know you're angry with me, Khalid,' she

said. 'But don't let it blind you to the way Dana and Allan feel. Hassan is a bad husband, be honest enough to admit that.'

'You dare to talk to me of honesty?'

'Why shouldn't I?'

'Because you don't know the meaning of the word. Everything you've said to me has been dishonest. Your innocence, your avowed love, your pretence at happiness. But you needn't continue with the act, nor is it necessary to sacrifice yourself.'

'Sacrifice myself?' she queried.

'By marrying me. Although perhaps marriage to a millionaire isn't such a sacrifice after all.'

'Don't be silly,' she said, refusing to take such a remark seriously. 'You can't doubt my love for you.'

'You never loved me,' he said abruptly. 'The scorn you felt for my ideas when we first met is still with you. But you pretended otherwise because of your brother.'

The scene was taking on a nightmare quality that Lorna refused to countenance.

'I'm very fond of my brother, but I'd never become your wife in order to help him. I regard marriage vows as sacred.'

'Then why are you advocating a divorce for Dana?'

'Because she was forced into her marriage and her vows meant nothing to her.'

'She made them and they still exist,' said Khalid. 'She is not only Hassan's wife by religious law but by Kuwaiti law as well.'

Seeing the implication behind his words, Lorna caught her breath. 'You mean you'd allow Hassan to take Amina away from Dana? How can you persist in following such outmoded traditions? Your mother was English, Khalid—for God's sake remember that.'

'I prefer to remember my father,' he replied. 'His people are my people. I have no other.'

'Don't argue with him,' said Allan, tight-lipped. 'I don't want you to ruin your chance of happiness because of me.'

'Allan's right,' said Dana, giving her brother a frightened look. 'If there's no other way that we can be together, I may have to leave Amina.'

Allan turned swiftly to Dana, but before he could speak she put her hand against his mouth and gave a slight shake of her head, as if to let him know this was something they would talk about later, when they were alone.

Watching them, Lorna knew her brother would never allow Dana to leave her baby. Though she said she was willing to do so, she was too deeply attached to her child to forget her, and the memory of Amina—were she to be left—would eventually sour their love.

Once again Lorna turned to Khalid, but he met her pleading look with a stony expression.

'We have nothing more to say to each other, Lorna. I wish you to leave my home.'

Speechlessly she went on staring at him, and Allan moved to her side and looked at Khalid fearlessly.

'I know how you feel about me, but you're

wrong to take it out on Lorna. She loves you.'

'I have already told you there is nothing more to say.'

Khalid turned his back on them both. His carriage was erect and his head was held high, giving him an air of hauteur that made him appear even more intransigent. Looking at the dark head Lorna knew it was hopeless to try to make him understand why she had not told him about Allan and Dana, or to make him believe that her love for him was genuine.

Their engagement was over. Their interlude of happiness was a brief one that would have to last her for the rest of her life. It was something she could not quite take in—as if the shock of events had numbed her—and she was glad of it, for it would enable her to get through the next few bitter days until she returned to England.

'What about tonight's party?'

Dana's question broke into the silence, and Khalid muttered an oath and swung round to them. Lorna saw from his expression that he had forgotten all about it.

'You must tell your uncle to cancel it,' she said.

Khalid glared at her. 'Commitments obviously mean as little to you as honesty. On no account will I let my uncle down. We are the guests of honour and we will attend the party and pretend we are still in love.'

'Is it a pretence?' Lorna asked, uncaring that Allan and Dana could hear her, and intent on trying to save her happiness. 'Is your love for me so shallow that it can dry up in a matter of minutes?'

'No,' he said bitterly. 'It is so deep that it will cut into my soul like a knife and leave a scar that will remain with me until I die.'

'Then how can you ask me to leave?'

'Because I would rather live with my torment than live with a woman I don't trust.'

She trembled so violently that she was grateful for the strength of Allan's arm around her.

'I can't go to the party,' she said shakily.

'You will,' Khalid commanded. 'Your brother still has a contract at our hospital, and if you don't do as I say, I will have it terminated and tell your B.M.A. why.'

'Your threats are invalid,' Allan cut in furiously. 'Dana was never my patient and I haven't done anything ethically wrong.'

'It will still harm your reputation if you were dismissed from your post before your time was up.'

Watching Khalid, Lorna knew he would carry out his threat. There was a glitter in his eyes she had never seen before, a harshness in his face that made it easy to liken him to the ruthless hawks so beloved of the Arabs.

She turned and gave her brother a resigned look.

'We must do as Khalid says. He's so obsessed with his own authority he can't see anyone else's point of view.'

The rest of the evening was a nightmare. The party, given in a magnificent modern villa outside the capital, was as lavish as Lorna had come to expect from Kuwaiti society, and listening to the specially imported American band and forcing

herself to nibble at the caviar and foie gras which
had been flown in from abroad, she understood
why Khalid had not wanted to let down his uncle.
What she did not understand was his ability to
pretend he was her loving fiancé.

He remained close to her side, giving her fre-
quent ardent glances and catching hold of her
hand from time to time and raising it to his lips.
No one could have guessed it was a charade, and
that within hours they would part, never to see
one another again.

'I can't go on with this,' she whispered shakily
as he drew her on to the dance floor.

'You have no choice.' His fingers dug deep into
her waist, though he kept a tender smile on his
lips.

'You're hurting me!' she protested.

'It is nothing to what I would like to do to you.'
His fingers dug deeper. 'Be my mistress, Lorna.
You can have all the money you want in exchange
for giving me your body.'

She gasped at his cruelty, but it was enough to
give her the impetus to carry on, and she followed
him as he guided her around the floor, even
managing to smile as she did so.

'Well,' he said into her ear, 'will you accept the
offer?'

'I'd rather be dead!'

'A pity. You are a beautiful creature and I will
always regret that I wasn't able to possess you.'

'Even if you went to bed with me, you wouldn't
possess me,' she said bitterly.

He did not answer, and for the rest of the evening he only spoke to her when other people were within earshot.

It was dawn before the party ended and she looked around for Allan to take her back to his apartment.

'You can't leave here with your brother,' Khalid said curtly. 'Everyone knows you are staying in my home, so you will have to come in my car. Allan can follow us, and when we're out of sight you can go with him.'

'My clothes——' she began.

'Before we left home I told the servants to pack your things and send the cases round to your brother's apartment.'

His ability to think so clearly in time of stress brought it home to her how strong his character was. It made her realise the futility of trying to make him listen to her side of the situation, and she silently climbed into his car and gripped her hands tightly together in an effort to stop herself bursting into tears. She felt the hardness of her engagement ring, which he had given her two days ago: an enormous diamond that had embarrassed her by its size until he had asked her to see it as but a small token of his love. Thinking of these words, she pulled the ring off, glad she was wearing none of the other jewellery he had given to her.

'Thanks for the loan of this,' she whispered. 'I'm sure you'll find someone else to give it to.'

'Keep it,' he shrugged. 'All the gifts I gave you are yours.'

'I want nothing from you.'

Silently he continued to drive, and glancing behind her she saw Allan's car through the rear screen window. A few hundred yards further on, Khalid stopped, and she opened the door and jumped out.

'You're a hard man,' she cried. 'One day I hope you'll regret what you've done.'

'I regret it now, but it is the will of Allah.'

'Rubbish! You——'

Khalid did not wait for her to complete the sentence. With a sharp screech of his wheels he set the car in motion and disappeared down the road in a cloud of dust.

Allan came to stand beside her, and even in the moonlight she saw the pallor of his face. Sympathy for him alleviated some of her own pain, and she put her hand on his arm and for an instant rested her head against his shoulder.

'I could kick myself for getting you into this mess,' he said in a strained voice. 'I'll wait until the morning and then go to see him. I'll force him to listen to me. He can't blame you because Dana and I love each other.'

'He blames me for not telling him,' she said shakily. 'You'll be wasting your time going to see him. He's not only a rigid man, Allan, he's a cruel one.'

'Yet you love him.'

'I love the man I thought he was. I don't love the Khalid I've just discovered him to be.'

In silence Allan led her to his car, and he did not speak again until he was unlocking the door of his apartment.

'I won't let Dana leave the baby,' he said. 'If
I did, she'd end up hating me.'

'If you leave, she might follow you.'

'Not if I make it clear that I won't see her
again.'

For the first time that evening Lorna could not
control her tears, nor did she make any attempt
to do so. She knew they would only bring her
momentary relief and that only time would ease
the depth of her pain.

Time and work; that was the best way to keep
Khalid out of her mind, if not out of her heart.

CHAPTER NINE

THE following morning Lorna tried to book a
flight home, but was told that the earliest seat
available was in two days. The thought of remaining here and possibly meeting people who
would wonder at her sudden departure kept her
confined to the apartment, though she telephoned
Ellen Driver to tell her she was leaving, and to
explain why.

But Ellen insisted that they meet.

'I'd come over to you,' she said briskly, 'but it
will do you more good to get out and know that

the world still exists—even if you think *you* don't.'

Lorna appreciated the comment and agreed to see Ellen, and shortly afterwards Allan's man-servant deposited her at the Drivers' apartment house.

She went up in the lift to the penthouse they occupied and found Ellen waiting by the door to greet her.

She hugged Lorna and drew her out on to the terrace. 'The whole of this was covered in sand this morning,' she grumbled, 'and it will be the same again by the evening. It even seeps under the doors and windows.'

'There's no way of stopping it,' Lorna replied. 'It's the same at Khalid's house.'

Her lips trembled as she uttered his name, and she wished desperately that she had not come here. She should have stayed at home where she could give way to her misery.

'No, you don't,' said Ellen. 'If you're going to cry, cry here, where I can help you to get over it.'

'I won't cry,' Lorna said with determination. 'He isn't worth it.'

'No man is worth it,' Ellen said cheerfully. 'But sit down and tell me the whole story.'

Lorna did so, her anger against Khalid rein-forced as she saw Ellen's expression. Yet when the woman spoke she was unusually philosophi-cal, though also pessimistic.

'Even if you had told Khalid about Dana and Allan the moment you got engaged to him, he wouldn't have changed his mind about them. I don't know him as well as Bill does, but he's very much his father's son. He believes in the sanctity of marriage.'

'But his father got divorced,' Lorna protested.

'And was always extremely bitter about it.'

'If Khalid's father was as obstinate as his son, I'm not surprised an Englishwoman wasn't happy with him!'

'Then you should be glad your engagement's off,' said Ellen.

'I probably will be,' Lorna said. 'But for the moment all she could think of was Khalid's arms around her and the warmth of his mouth as it had taken possession of hers. His body had promised untold delights, but they were delights she would never experience with him.

'He's a handsome brute,' Ellen said into the silence. 'But you'll meet another man some day who'll help you to forget him. Now how about sharing a cheese omelette with me? I bet you haven't eaten anything all day.'

'I haven't,' Lorna confessed, and followed her friend into the resplendent modern kitchen.

Later, as they sipped their coffee on the terrace, Ellen decided to call Allan at the hospital and suggest he joined them for dinner. He accepted gratefully, knowing that if he and Lorna remained alone together they would make each other more miserable than they already were.

No one shied away from talking about the situation, and Bob echoed Ellen's opinion in saying that even if Lorna had told Khalid the truth as soon as she had become engaged to him, it would have made no difference to his attitude towards his sister's marriage.

'Possibly not,' Allan agreed. 'But it would have made a difference to Lorna. At least she and Khalid would still be engaged.'

'I don't think Lorna would have married him if he'd gone on being so obstinate about Dana and you,' Ellen intervened.

It was something Lorna had never considered, and she was not sure if Ellen was right.

'Khalid's not a bad guy,' Bill said. 'It's only when it comes to women that he thinks like an Arab.'

'The Koran may see women as second-class citizens, but the Bible doesn't,' Allan pointed out. 'And Khalid is a Christian.'

'He's also a Kuwaiti,' Bill said whimsically.

'This is supposed to be the most progressive state in the Gulf for women,' said Lorna, echoing one of Khalid's remarks to her.

'Don't you believe it,' Ellen replied. 'They may have the vote, and even a women's movement, but they're merely status symbols. This is a man's country and you'd do well not to forget it. Kuwaiti family life is a mockery of freedom, and in some ways it's more segregated and harsher than anywhere else.' She stopped to sip at her coffee. 'Just look at the *diwania*. Where else would a husband be allowed a room of his own with a separate entrance, which he uses exclusively for entertaining other men?'

'Truly?' Lorna asked.

'Truly. It's supposed to be a place where he can gossip and play cards, but I suspect he plays a lot of other games there too!'

'It's all perfectly innocent,' her husband protested. 'They may import an occasional belly dancer for entertainment, but that's *all*.' His eyes lit up mischievously. 'It might even catch on in the States, if only someone had the nerve to introduce it!'

'If you start behaving like a Kuwaiti husband,' Ellen warned, 'I'll start spending your money like a Kuwaiti wife!'

The Drivers' playful banter did wonders for Lorna and Allan, and for a while at least they were able to forget their own troubles.

They were standing in the hallway, ready to leave, when the telephone rang. Bill answered it and then handed it to Allan.

'It's the hospital,' he said.

Allan frowned. 'I'm not on call tonight.' He spoke into the receiver, then stopped and listened, his colour swiftly receding. 'It's Dana,' he muttered, setting down the phone. 'She's crashed her car into a tree.'

'She doesn't drive,' Lorna cried.

Allan closed his eyes, then opened them again. They were opaque with shock. 'She tried to kill herself. That was Khalid on the phone. He was speaking from the hospital. She's barely conscious, but she's asking for me.'

'I'll drive you,' Bill said at once, and within a minute they were on their way, moving as fast as the bumper-to-bumper traffic would allow.

Lorna had been into the hospital several times since coming to Kuwait, but as always she marvelled at its luxuriousness, and could not understand why the Kuwaitis still chose to come to London for their operations. Perhaps they regarded it as a fashionable thing to do—the Arab equivalent of keeping up with the Joneses.

As she and the Drivers stepped out on to the fourth floor, she saw Khalid by the reception desk, talking to one of the nurses. Lorna had a chance to study him for a brief instant before he noticed them, and saw that in less than twenty-four hours he had aged ten years. His face was gaunt and hollow, his eyes lifeless. Yet she did not try to make herself believe it was on her own account. If he was suffering, it was because of Dana. Reiterating this thought to herself, she was able to look at him with composure, as he saw her and strode over.

'Where's your brother?' he demanded.

'He rushed up ahead of us. He must have walked past you.'

'Maybe he went directly to the operating theatre,' Khalid said huskily.

'How bad is she?' Ellen asked.

Khalid's eyes glittered with moisture and he bit hard on his lower lip.

'Are you afraid to cry?' Lorna flared, beyond caring what she said to him. 'Or won't your conscience let you? You're as guilty of hurting Dana as if you'd crashed the car into her!'

'Lorna, don't.' Ellen caught her arm and drew her into one of the waiting rooms. 'Telling Khalid

what you think of him isn't going to help anyone.
All we can do is pray for Dana.'

Lorna sank down on a chair and buried her head
in her hands. She wanted to go to the operating
theatre, but knew she would not be allowed in,
regardless of her professional status. Only Allan
could do that, and since he was already there, they
would get first-hand information when he returned.

There was a quiet movement beside her and
she looked up into Khalid's blue eyes. They were
red-rimmed, but she felt no sympathy for him. He
deserved to suffer. The only pity was that other
people had to suffer with him.

'Does your stepmother know?' she asked.

'Yes. She wanted to come here, but I wouldn't
let her.'

'She's Dana's mother,' Lorna said bitterly. 'She
has a right to be with her daughter. Or aren't
women supposed to be capable of feeling sorrow?'

Deep hurt flashed across Khalid's face. 'Do you
think I wouldn't let her come here because she's
a woman? Is that how badly you think of me?'

'I'm trying not to think of you. All my thoughts
are with Dana.'

'So are mine.' He took the seat next to her. 'I
wouldn't let my stepmother come here because
she went into a state of shock and had to be
sedated.'

'I see.' Lorna still felt too bitterly towards him
to apologise. 'Does Hassan know?'

'He's waiting by the telephone in London. He
wanted to fly out immediately, but I wouldn't let

him. I didn't want him to come here and see Allan
with her. If he did, he'd soon guess what's been
going on.'

'Still determined to preserve an empty marriage, aren't you?' Lorna accused.

'I am intent on preserving my sister's good
name. If she dies, I don't want there to be any
scandal surrounding her.'

'And if she lives?'

Khalid said nothing. Like a statue he sat beside
her. He was wearing the white dashdasha and it
forcibly brought his foreignness home to her. She
had been crazy to think they could be happy together.

'There's no point in us sitting here and waiting
like this,' Bob Driver said suddenly. 'I suggest you
two ladies ask one of the nurses where you can get
some coffee, and Khalid and I will go down to the
car. I brought some brandy with me, and he looks
as if he can do with a stiff drink.'

'I want nothing,' Khalid said tonelessly.

'Well, I do,' the American replied. 'And as your
lawyer, I insist you take my advice and have one
with me.'

Like an automaton Khalid rose, and the two
men went out.

'He's taking it very badly,' Ellen commented as
soon as they were alone.

'Conscience,' Lorna retorted.

'Maybe.' Ellen sighed. 'Poor Dana! She must
really love your brother to do a stupid thing like
this.'

'And where will it leave her if she recovers?'

Lorna asked. 'Back at square one. It hasn't solved a thing.'

'You never know. Khalid might have a change of heart and allow her to divorce Hassan.'

'At this moment he'd probably agree to anything. But he'll change his mind if she gets better. I've seen it happen so many times—families who forget their grievances over the sick-bed of a loved one, and then fall out again when the patient recovers. And if they don't, and die, they usually end up fighting over the will.'

'Nursing has made you cynical,' sighed Ellen.

'It's made me realistic.'

'Does that mean you still intend leaving tomorrow?'

'I won't go until Dana's off the danger list,' Lorna told her.

'And then you'll leave?'

'There won't be any reason for me to stay.'

Ellen hesitated. 'I'm sure that what's happened tonight will make Khalid see things differently. He may want you back.'

'Out of a belated sense of guilt? I can just see into his mind now,' Lorna said bitterly. 'Making a pact with God that if He'll let Dana recover——'

'Don't talk like that,' Ellen interrupted.

'Then don't talk to me about Khalid. I don't mean to be rude, Ellen, but some things are better left unsaid.'

Neither of them spoke again and Ellen left the waiting room and returned shortly afterwards with a tray of coffee and biscuits. Lorna drank the coffee but could not eat anything, and they were sitting in silence once again when the men returned. The brandy Khalid had drunk had brought some colour back into his skin, and he no longer blended into his white dashdasha, but the lines were still heavly marked on his face and his eyes were bleak.

The hours slowly ticked away and it was three a.m. before Allan came in to tell them Dana would live.

'I'm staying beside her tonight,' he said. 'She's in intensive care and we'll keep her there for the next twenty-four hours.'

Khalid looked as though he wanted to speak, but even when he opened his lips, no words came out. He put his hand to his face and closed his eyes, and Allan moved over and spoke softly to him, so that no one else could hear.

Lorna did not know what her brother said, but it had the effect of making Khalid straighten and look more composed. Allan is more forgiving than I am, she thought wryly, and still could not bring herself to make any gesture of sympathy to the man whom she both loved and despised.

'If Allan's going to stay at the hospital, why don't you come home with us?' Ellen asked her.

'I'd rather go back to the apartment,' Lorna murmured, and refused to look in Khalid's direction as they left the hospital and went to their respective cars.

It was three days later before Lorna saw Khalid again, and then it was only as she was walking down the corridor to Dana's room, and he was coming out of it. He still looked haggard, but it in no way detracted from his looks. Indeed it enhanced them, giving his eyes greater depth and drawing attention to the fine cut of his mouth.

'Dana will be delighted to see you,' he said. 'She was just asking about you.'

'She knew from Allan that I hadn't gone home yet,' Lorna said stiffly. 'I wanted to see her first.'

'And then you're leaving?'

'Yes.'

'You wouldn't consider staying on for a while as her companion?'

'I'm sure you'd feel happier if your sister had an Arab woman as her companion,' Lorna said icily. 'Someone who'd be less likely to corrupt her with liberated ideas of being happy with one's husband.'

She went to walk past him, but he put out his hand and detained her. 'Try not to think bitterly of me, Lorna. I——'

'I don't think of you at all,' she lied. 'I'm amazed at how quickly you've come to mean nothing to me. I guess I must have been bowled over by your glamour and money after all, but coming to the hospital each day has given me back my old perspective.'

Khalid's hand dropped away from her. 'They say the tongue of a woman can kill quicker than the tongue of a serpent,' he said, 'and you are proving the sages right.'

Not looking at him, she walked away, her eyes so blinded by tears that it was only pure chance that she stopped in front of Dana's room.

One sight of her friend put her own personal

thoughts out of her mind, for the girl was covered in bandages and had a leg and an arm in traction. But she managed to smile a greeting and Lorna went over to kiss her, then drew a chair close to the bed.

'Khalid's just left,' Dana whispered.

'I know, I saw him.'

'You spoke to him?'

'Of course.'

'Are you. . . . Will you come together again?'

'No.' Lorna made her voice light. 'That's all in the past. I'm going back to London.'

'Hassan isn't coming here,' said Dana. 'Khalid didn't tell him how badly injured I was. He was afraid that if Hassan came here he'd guess the way Allan and I feel about each other.' The brown eyes were lambent with tears. 'Lying here alone like this has made me give much more thought to my brother's point of view. Although I don't agree with it, I can see why he behaves this way. Tradition, and the wishes of our father, mean everything to him, and my father would never have allowed me to leave Hassan. When his own marriage to Khalid's mother ended, he completely abandoned all his Western ideas and became the most devout Muslim.'

'Yet he allowed Khalid to be educated in the West,' said Lorna.

'Because he wanted the best education for him. But Khalid always had an Arab companion with him when he was abroad.'

This further insight into Khalid's upbringing made Lorna even more astonished that he could

have forgotten his heritage sufficiently to consider
marrying her, and she began to appreciate how
strong his desire for her had been. But it was desire, not love, she reminded herself, for love would
have brought understanding of the predicament
she had been in with Allan.

'Don't go back to London,' Dana broke into
her thoughts. 'Stay another few weeks.'

'It's impossible. I have a job waiting for me,'
she lied. 'I telephoned the Matron of my old hospital in London just before you had your accident,
and she agreed to take me back.'

Though Dana looked sceptical she did not
argue, and Lorna was thankful for it.

The day before her departure she decided it
would be impolite to leave Kuwait without saying goodbye to Madam al Hashib. She knew from
Allan that Khalid had flown to London on business, and with no fear of running into him, she
went to the villa.

The woman looked pleased to see her, and
though her English was poor, she seemed more
fluent in it now that she was alone with Lorna
than when her stepson or daughter had been
present.

'Khalid told me all,' she said, after greetings
were made and coffee and sweetmeats had been
served. 'I sorry for Dana. But my parents chose
husband for me, and I happy.'

'Because your husband was a good man,' Lorna
said. 'But Dana's husband is quite different, and
she's terribly unhappy with him.'

'She must accept. Khalid he happy too, when he marry.'

Lorna swallowed hard. 'Is . . . is Khalid getting married?'

'Soon. I like you, but is better he marry Kuwaiti girl. He agree I find bride for him.'

Because of the woman's limited English, Lorna was not sure whether he had already agreed or his stepmother was assuming he would, and it was not until she went to say goodbye to Dana that she was able to clarify the mystery.

'Mother was referring to Najat Rahman,' Dana answered. 'Najat's father is her first cousin and he has been a business competitor of Khalid's for years. Her greatest wish has been to unite the two families in marriage. It was my father's wish too.'

'I'm surprised Khalid didn't marry her years ago. If he was such a dutiful son. . . .'

'Najat was too young. She's only seventeen now.'

Lorna sniffed. 'She sounds far more suitable than I would have been.'

'She is,' said Dana, with what Lorna considered singular lack of tact. 'And she's awfully pretty. But childish and docile.'

'Just right for your brother.'

'I'm pleased to see you can joke about it,' commented Dana.

'Why shouldn't I? I've told you, the past is past.'

Dana nodded. 'Perhaps it won't turn out as dreary for Khalid as I used to think. With Najat as his wife he won't be involved emotionally, so he won't be unhappy. He'll have lots of affairs— the way Hassan does.'

Lorna almost choked.

'If you're advocating marriage Kuwaiti style for your brother, it's a pity you can't be happy with Kuwaiti style marriage yourself,' she said.

'I might be, if I was allowed the same freedom. Or if I weren't desperately in love with your hard-headed brother. You know he's asked to be released from his contract and intends to return to England?'

Lorna nodded. Allan had told her of his intention and she had not argued him out of it, deciding he was taking the best course of action.

'Khalid told me he is sending Hassan to New York,' Dana continued. 'He's gone to London to arrange it now.'

'At least you won't bump into Allan there,' said Lorna.

'That's why Khalid's moving us,' Dana replied bleakly. 'I begged him to put pressure on Hassan to set me free, but he refused even to discuss it.'

Lorna bit her lip. If only Ellen could hear Dana she would no longer call Lorna a cynic for the opinions she had expressed the other night. Khalid was proving them all too true.

'You won't do anything foolish again, will you?' she asked.

'No,' Dana said glumly. 'I didn't intend to commit suicide last weekend either. I was just so beside myself with misery that I wanted to go for a drive. I never officially passed my test when I was in London, but I did have half a dozen lessons.'

'And you've paid for the most expensive lesson of all,' Lorna commented, looking at the bandaged arm and leg. 'Concentrate on your baby and forget everything else.'

'I can never forget Allan. Even if he marries someone else, I will always love him.'

There was nothing Lorna could say to this. From the way Allan had spoken to her, she could not imagine him falling in love with another girl, yet she knew that when one was young the deepest wounds could heal, and it was more than conceivable that her brother would find, if not great happiness, at least contentment with someone else. As she herself would hope to do in the future.

Her final parting from Dana was sad for both of them, but they had both suffered too deep a shock to cry, and it was only when Lorna was on the plane that she could no longer control her tears.

How different her departure was from her arrival! There was no private jet, no Concorde and no VIP treatment. Yet it was not these luxuries that she missed, but Khalid's dark, virile presence, and the memory of him occupied all her thoughts during the long journey back to England.

CHAPTER TEN

'PHONE call for you, Sister.'

Chrissy Wilson, a cheeky young student nurse, popped her head round the door of the private room where Lorna was listening to the woes of her patient. Pleased to have a valid excuse to leave the spoiled elderly woman without hurting her feelings, she returned to her well-furnished office at the end of the corridor. Even the staff had excellent accommodation in this most exclusive of private clinics.

'Just making sure you haven't forgotten our dinner date for tonight,' a plummy male voice reminded her.

'Of course I haven't forgotten,' Lorna lied, thankful she had not made another date for this evening. 'What time are you picking me up?'

'At eight-thirty. I've booked a table at the Elephant.'

At least the evening wouldn't be a complete waste, she thought, as she drove back to her flat to change. Rupert Melville was not her ideal escort —no one was, after Khalid—but at least he was amusing, fairly intelligent and always took her to her favourite restaurants.

She had been introduced to him at a match-making dinner party given by one of her mother's friends, and though she had at first refused to go out with him, his persistence finally won the day.

Having taken the plunge and accepted an invitation from a man, she found it easy to accept more, and hoped she would eventually meet some-one who would make her heart beat just that little bit faster. But for the moment Khalid was still too clear in her mind, and she compared everyone with him; finding their kisses too inexpert, their hold too rough, their touch too heavy.

For a dominant man, Khalid had been a sensi-tive lover. Not her lover in the real sense of the word, but as near to it as he had allowed himself to come. She found herself regretting the control he had placed upon their behaviour; at least if she had given herself to him she would have that much more to remember.

Promptly at eight-thirty she was waiting for Rupert, wearing one of the many dresses Khalid had insisted on buying her as part of her trous-seau. Unpacking them all in London she had been sorely tempted to give them away, afraid of the memories they would evoke each time she wore them. But sense had won the day, and she had forced herself to see them only as beautiful gar-ments which she would never have been able to afford had she been buying them herself.

Tonight her choice was one of the last dresses Khalid had bought her. Of floating chiffon, it dis-guised the weight she had lost since returning home, and the delicate pink colour lessened the shadows below her cheekbones and the darker ones that lay below her eyes.

Rupert did his best to entertain her, but for some reason Khalid seemed closer than ever, and by the time she returned home she was so depressed that she had to take a sleeping pill.

In consequence she was late getting up, and staring at her haggard face in the mirror, determined to snap out of the self-pitying mood she had been in since her return. Think positive, she told her reflection, and for pity's sake stop thinking about Khalid. Tightening her belt a notch, she went into the tiny kitchenette she shared with her friend Ann.

'Just in time for a cup of cold coffee,' Ann remarked cheerfully. 'Does oversleeping imply that you had a particularly good evening?'

'No.'

'Then how come you're looking less miserable?'

'I think I'm finally getting over Khalid,' Lorna told her.

'Pigs might fly if their bottoms weren't so heavy,' Ann answered drily.

'What does that mean?'

'It means I don't believe in miracles.'

Lorna smiled. 'But it's true. I am getting over him. And to prove it, I'll have my hair re-styled. He always liked it long, so I'll have it cut short.'

'That sounds more like an act of defiance than proof that you're getting over him. But at least it's a start.' Ann eyed her. 'Don't have it completely shorn.'

There was a rattle from the postman at the

front door, and Ann rose to collect the letters.

'Anything for me from Allan?' Lorna asked hopefully. He hadn't written for a few weeks, not since informing her that his replacement at the Saud Hospital had been delayed.

'Nothing except bills—but they're all for me, so you can still afford to tootle off to Mayfair and get your locks shorn.'

Several hours later Lorna emerged from Sassoon's Bond Street salon with the latest Vidal creation. It gave her a different kind of beauty and she was delighted by it. Her hair fell sleekly to the lobes of her ears and then curled upwards in wispy fronds. Her cool, sophisticated appearance had gone, and was now replaced by a more gamine charm. She might not feel like a new woman yet, but she had taken the first steps towards it.

'I like it,' Marcia Reed, her co-floor supervisor, remarked as she entered their shared office. 'You'll have all the male temperatures rising!'

Lorna smiled her thanks. 'Anything new?'

'One emergency admittance. A young Arab woman—suspected broken ankle. Apparently she's on her honeymoon, and her husband wants her out of here as quickly as possible.'

They looked at each other and laughed.

'Dr Simpson's her physician,' Marcia added. 'He's due in soon to see the X-rays.'

Lorna settled down to read some reports before doing her rounds, but no sooner had she opened a folder when there was a tap at the door.

'Dr Simpson's here to see the new patient,

Sister,' a young staff nurse informed her.

Lorna stood up. 'Is the surgeon with him?'

'No. Only a dishy-looking man—the husband, I think.'

Lorna walked briskly towards the private ward. The door of the room was shut, but she saw through the small glass pane, and her steps faltered.

Next to the bed, watching with concern as the specialist held an X-ray plate up to the light, stood Khalid.

The blood drained from Lorna's face. So he had finally married Najat! She went on staring at him. How handsome he looked, and how exactly the way she so often dreamed of him. In his well-fitting navy suit he seemed the epitome of charm, instead of an autocrat used to giving orders and having them obeyed. Yet regardless of what he wore, the man beneath the clothes remained the same.

'Anything wrong, Sister?' A nurse walking past stopped to look at her.

Lorna wanted to turn tail and run, but if she did, the news of it would be all over the hospital in an hour. With an effort she controlled herself.

'No,' she said, and with an effort drew a deep breath, pushed open the door and went inside.

Three pairs of eyes swivelled in her direction, although it was left to the doctor to speak.

'Good morning, Sister. Nothing too complicated here, I'm glad to say. Just a simple fracture that we can deal with if you'll telephone the Theatre.'

'I'll arrange it immediately, sir.' Lorna ignored

Khalid, and wished she could also ignore the very pretty doe-eyed young girl lying on the bed. She could have passed for Dana's sister, having the same luscious dark-haired looks. However, she seemed extremely nervous and Lorna moved to the side of the bed, glad that it took her even further away from Khalid, who was by the window.

'You've nothing to be afraid of,' she said in her most professionally soothing voice. 'You'll be back in this room within half an hour and you can be out of here this afternoon.'

'She doesn't understand English,' the surgeon murmured quietly, and gave the young girl a beaming smile.

Lorna had never known Dr Simpson to display such warmth, and wondered cynically whether the al Hashib name had something to do with it. She turned towards the door.

'I'll phone the Theatre,' she murmured, 'and ask them to send up a porter with a wheelchair.'

She had arranged it and was back in her office, sipping a cup of coffee and wishing it were a stiff drink when the door opened without a warning knock and Khalid came in.

With a deep sense of inevitability she waited for him to speak. How blue his eyes were! Her bones seemed to melt and her breathing was ragged. She had known he would seek her out the moment his wife had been wheeled away, and she wondered if he were a sadist or merely curious to know how she now felt about him.

'You've had your hair cut,' he said.

His comment was so unexpected that she was at a loss for words.

'It suits you,' he went on. 'You look more beautiful than ever.'

He came closer to the desk and she was glad she was sitting down; if she hadn't she would have fallen.

'You've lost weight,' he went on, 'and there are shadows under your eyes.'

'Are you making an inventory of me?' Lorna finally found her voice and, with it, her temper. 'I've no time to——'

'When are you off duty?' he interrupted. 'I want to talk to you.'

'Well, I don't want to talk to you.'

'I don't blame you,' he said. 'But you'll have to talk to me anyway.'

'I won't!'

'Please,' he pleaded. 'I know you have been terribly hurt, but so was I.'

'Poor Khalid!' she taunted.

'Stupid Khalid,' he replied. 'I behaved like a maniac over you and Dana.'

Surprise kept her silent. She dared not think what he meant in case she put the wrong interpretation on it. She felt his eyes upon her. Their blue was now intensified, glowing with a passion that set her body aflame. She ached to hold him close, to feel him tremble the way he always did when she was near him. Yet none of these thoughts showed on her face, which remained as cool as an angel's carved in stone.

'I love you,' Khalid said huskily. 'That's what I'm trying to tell you. I want you to be my wife.'

She was not sure she had heard correctly. Had he changed his religion in order to marry Najat, and was he now seeing Lorna as part of his harem?

'Well?' he asked. 'Haven't you anything to say?'

'Only that my answer is no, and that you're still behaving like a maniac if you think I'll agree.'

The colour seeped from his skin and she had a swift image of him as he had been the night that Dana's life had hung in the balance. Yet why should he look so bereft now? She refused to believe he genuinely loved her. Had he done, he would never have married Najat.

'Do you honestly see me as part of your harem?' she burst out. 'Or do you plan to set me up in a house in London and visit me when you come over from Kuwait? I don't know what rights second wives have, but——'

'Second wives?' he cut in. 'You think I am married to Najat?'

'Don't tell me she's your mistress too!'

'I wouldn't,' he said with infuriating calm. 'She is definitely a wife, though not mine. She is married to Hassan.'

Lorna was too astounded to speak. She swallowed hard. 'Are you . . . are you telling me Dana and Hassan are divorced?'

'Yes.' He came round the side of the desk, but

seeing her shrink back in the chair, he stopped.
'Don't be frightened of me, Lorna. I won't touch
you if you don't want me.'

She drew a deep breath and ignored what he had
said. 'Where's Dana? And what's happened with
Allan? He wrote to me two weeks ago, but he
never said a word about any divorce.'

'Because he didn't know of it. Nobody knew—
not even Dana herself. I arranged it all with Hassan.'

This behaviour seemed so typical of Khalid
that Lorna felt hysterical amusement rising up in
her. Only this man would have the gall to arrange
for his sister's divorce without letting his sister
know. He was as likely to marry her off to someone else in the same way.

Suspiciously she regarded him. 'I assume you've
already picked out her next husband?'

'Dana's done that for herself, as you damn well
know.' Khalid's temper was less equable now.
'Stop playing with me, Lorna. I've had two
months of hell trying to work things out, and
forcing myself not to let you know what was going on until I'd got it all settled.'

'Settled?' she echoed.

'Hassan remarried and is sufficiently pleased
with himself to let Dana keep Amina.'

'No!' Lorna cried, and jumped up so quickly
that the chair fell back. Disregarding it, she flung
herself into Khalid's arms, a place where she had
never expected to be again.

'Why didn't you tell me what you were doing?' she cried.

'I was afraid to, in case Hassan wouldn't do as I wanted. He isn't as easy to deal with as you think. I know I have authority over him in business, but *he* has authority over Amina, and he was determined to exercise it to his best advantage.'

'You mean he blackmailed you?'

Khalid nodded. 'But I'd have paid any price to give myself the right to come back to you.'

His hold on her tightened and she felt the heavy beat of his heart. His mouth sought hers hungrily and she responded to him wildly.

Again and again they kissed, and even when he finally lifted his head he did not release her, but rested his cheek upon her own, his breath warm on her skin. His thin silk suit did little to disguise the urgency of his desire, and aware that she felt it, he gave a half sigh.

'Do I need to ask you again to marry me?' he said.

'What a silly question!' She caressed the back of his neck, loving the feel of his soft hair. 'As soon as you like, darling.'

'Is the end of the week too soon?'

'No.' She pulled slightly back from him. 'I suppose you'll want us to be married in Kuwait?'

'No. I thought you would like to be married here.' He paused, then said: 'There's something else I have to tell you, but I'd rather wait until this evening.'

His gravity faintly disquieted her, and she might not have been able to contain her curiosity if one of her nurses hadn't come in to say the patient was back from the Theatre, with her foot set in plaster.

This reminded Lorna to ask Khalid why he had come here with Najat, instead of Hassan.

'Because the three of us were at London Airport. I had just flown in from Kuwait and Hassan and Najat met me at the airport. They were on their way to America. Then Najat fell on the steps of the plane, and since it was essential for Hassan to attend a meeting in New York, he asked me to take care of her.'

'Otherwise you'd be on your way to New York too?'

He gave her a none too gentle shake.

'I was on my way here. Bringing Najat along with me was simple. But no more explanations. I'll see you tonight.'

He was at the door when she called him, and he turned to look at her, one dark eyebrow raised.

'You don't know where I live, Khalid.'

'I know your address and your phone number. I know the hours you are on duty and also that you are only working here on a temporary basis until you get your old job back at the hospital.'

She gave a shaky laugh. 'Have you been having me watched?'

'Yes,' he said slowly. 'If you had gone out with the same man more than three times, I would have flown here to see you regardless of how my negotiations were going with Hassan.'

'I see.' She trembled at the suppressed violence in his voice. 'You're very possessive, aren't you?'

'You are my life, Lorna. When I remembered

how cruel I was to you because of your loyalty to your brother. . . .'

'You've more than made up for it,' she said. 'Don't be humble, Khalid, or I won't know you.'

His smile was brief and the door closed on him. Left alone, Lorna resisted the urge to sit at her desk and think of the future. There was work to do first. Tonight was hers and Khalid's.

Because she was on late call, it was eight o'clock before she was free, and nine o'clock before she was at home waiting for Khalid. Hearing of his arrival, Ann had tactfully made herself scarce, saying she would spend the night with a friend, an offer which Lorna had accepted, knowing that if Khalid made love to her here, she would not let him leave her.

His step on the stairs sent her racing to the door, and she opened it before he could ring. It was a good thing she did, for he was laden with champagne and a wicker basket which unpacked to disclose caviar, cold lobster and fresh strawberries.

'I knew you wouldn't have eaten,' he explained, 'and I was too restless to eat either, until I'd seen you again.'

In the bright light of the living-room she could see he hadn't eaten much for weeks, for though he looked happy, his face was bone-thin. Tenderness welled up in her and with a murmur she clasped him close and pressed her mouth to his temple.

'You said you had something to tell me,' she whispered.

'Later,' he replied. 'First we will eat.'

They did so in the kitchen, Khalid looking incongruously elegant among the blue and white formica cabinets. But it was not until the meal was over and they were seated in the lounge that he finally quieted her curiosity.

'Two days after I asked you to marry me,' he began, 'Bob Driver told me that my father had given him a letter before he died, and instructed him only to let me have it if I married a Western woman. I asked Bob to let me have it, but he was under orders not to do so until the night before my marriage.'

'You must have been awfully curious,' she said, her own curiosity mounting.

'I was. But Bob wouldn't break his orders. When I parted from you he naturally felt vindicated about having stuck to his principles, though it still left me wondering what my father had written.'

'So that's why you're marrying me,' she laughed. 'Just to get that letter!'

'How clever of you to guess.' He smiled, but it was not with his eyes, which remained serious. 'When I told Bob I was flying here to marry you, he gave me the letter the day I left Kuwait.'

Khalid paused, and was silent for so long that Lorna thought he had changed his mind about telling her the contents, or that what he had to say was so difficult that he did not know how to begin.

'The letter was such a shock to me that even now I can hardly believe it,' he went on finally.

'Yet I know it is true, and it makes me love my father even more. For it shows how deep his love was for me.'

'But you never doubted that.'

'I never doubted that I was his son, either,' Khalid said gruffly. 'But it seems I'm not.'

Lorna couldn't believe she had heard correctly. 'You're not. . . .'

'No. Apparently my mother was married to an Englishman before, an officer in the army who was killed in action eight months before I was born. She had known my father—I still think of him that way,' he added, 'before her first marriage, and though he was in love with her, she did not return his feelings. Then, when she was widowed and found herself with a small pension and a baby on the way, she agreed to marry Achmed al Hashib.'

'You mean he was willing to take someone else's child and bring it up as his own?'

'I don't think he thought that far ahead. He loved my mother so much that he couldn't think of anything else. By the time he realised the marriage wasn't working out, he had grown to regard me as his own child. If he had had a son by his second marriage, I am sure he would have told me the truth earlier, but after Dana was born my stepmother couldn't have any more children.'

'What made your father leave a letter for you? I mean, if he didn't want to tell you the truth when he was alive, why do so afterwards?'

'I would never have learned the truth had I married an Arab. But if I married a Westerner he considered it his duty to let me know I was an Englishman, so that if I wished, my children could be English too. It would make no difference to the inheritance I had received from him, nor from my remaining head of the al Hashib family —if that was what I still wanted. But he felt he had to tell me the truth, so that if my future wife wanted me to live elsewhere, I would feel free to do so without a guilty conscience.'

It was not difficult for Lorna to understand the conflict that Khalid's stepfather had gone through in order to write such a letter, and she began to appreciate the generous soul of the man, and to understand why Khalid had loved him so deeply.

'It's your decision now, Lorna,' Khalid said. 'The name of my real father is Winters, Edmund Morley Winters. It's up to you to choose which name I should take.'

'You would let *me* decide such a thing?'

'It's the least I can do after the wounding things I said to you.'

'I could never make such a decision,' she declared. 'You are the only one who can do it.'

He walked over to the window, as if only by standing some distance away from her could he marshal his thoughts.

'Who rules me, Lorna? My heart or my head?' There was wry humour in his voice. 'Would it surprise you to know that they both say the same thing?'

'No,' she said instantly. 'Because I expected it. You wouldn't be the man I love if you could think otherwise.'

'Then you know what I wish to do?'

'I know what's the right thing to do, and since you always want to do the right thing. . . .'

With a groan he returned to her and caught her hands.

'The al Hashibs are the only family I have known. Though Edmund Winters was no doubt an admirable man, he is a stranger to me. It is Achmed al Hashib who gave me love and his name; who took me in when my mother discarded me, and who truly regarded me as his own child. To give up his name would be to discard that love, and I would rather cut off my right hand.'

Lorna drew his hand up to her face and pressed her lips against it. 'I love your hand,' she murmured, 'and I want you to keep it.' Momentarily she held herself away from him. 'Have you told anyone else the truth?'

'You are the first to know.'

'Then let me be the last.'

This time she could not evade his urgent mouth, nor did she want to, and she gave herself up to the delight of his touch. His hands were gentle on her, almost as if he were still not sure of her response, and she was the one who made the advances until, fired by her passion, he became the master once again.

The depth of his kisses intensified, and he slipped her dress from her shoulders and let his mouth travel along the sloping curve of her breasts. They were swollen with desire for him, and he buried his face in the shadowy cleft between them.

Then with a muffled groan, he pushed her away. 'Don't tempt me, Lorna. I'm only human.'

'So am I,' she said, 'which is why Ann isn't coming back tonight!'

His eyes darkened, but he still remained motionless. 'I'm willing to wait for you, my darling.'

'Why should you?' she asked, 'when I am more than willing.'

Rising to her feet, she pulled him up, and arms entwined they walked towards the bedroom.

They were at the door when he stopped.

'No,' he said firmly. 'I will not. The al Hashib men have always waited to possess their wives until their wedding night and——'

'And as your father's son you wish to do the same,' Lorna finished for him, and gently led him to the front door. 'You're right, Khalid. But then you always are.'

'I'll have that typed out and get you to sign it,' he chuckled as he kissed her brow. 'Until the day after tomorrow, my golden girl—when we will never have to part again.'

A MIDEASTERN DELIGHT

Lorna and Kahlid sit down one evening to a delicious Arabic feast of stuffed vine leaves (also called grape leaves). We thought readers might enjoy sampling for themselves this flavorful and simple dish, and following is a recipe kindly provided by one of our Harlequin editors.

Ingredients:

    50 vine leaves, soaked in brine (may
        be purchased at Mideastern
        speciality food stores)
     1 lb. lean ground beef or lamb
     1 cup rice, raw
     1 tsp. salt
        fresh ground pepper to taste
    ¼ tsp. garlic powder

Method:

Rinse leaves thoroughly in cold water. Squeeze out moisture and set aside. In a bowl, combine meat, rice, salt, pepper and garlic. Spoon out a dollop of meat mixture onto a vine leaf. Roll leaf with mixture inside until it has the size and shape of a cigar. Continue stuffing remaining leaves until all of mixture is used. Layer stuffed leaves in a large saucepan. Firmly press a heavy metal plate (a lid of a slightly smaller saucepan will do) over leaves, and do not remove. Add just enough water to reach the edges of the plate. Bring to a boil, then cover large saucepan and simmer for 35 minutes. Remove cover and plate, and squeeze the juice of two lemons over the leaves. Delicious served with side helpings of plain yogurt.